EARTHLORD

Second of the De Danann Tales

Michael Scott

D1336179

WOLFHOUND PRESS
IRISH AMERICAN BOOK COMPANY (IABC)

This edition reprinted 1997
First published 1992 by
WOLFHOUND PRESS
68 Mountjoy Square
Dublin 1

Wolfhound Press receives financial assistance from The Arts
Council/ An Chomhairle Ealaíon, Dublin, Ireland.

British Library Cataloguing in Publication Data
Scott, Michael, *1959—*
    Earthlord. — (De Danann Tales Series)
    I. Title II. Series
    823.914 [J]

    ISBN 0-86327-343-2

This book is fiction. All characters, incidents and names have no
connection with any persons living or dead. Any apparent resemblance is purely coincidental.

Published in the U.S. and Canada by
Irish American Book Company (IABC)
6309 Monarch Park Place, Niwot, Colorado 80503
Phone 303 530 1352 Fax 303 530 4488

For Courtney and Piers.

Cover design and illustration: Peter Haigh
Map: Aileen Caffrey
Typesetting: Wolfhound Press
Printed in Great Britain by Cox & Wyman Ltd., Reading, Berkshire.

Contents

	Prologue	6
1	The Beast in the Bushes	7
2	The Market	12
3	The Pendants	17
4	The Sea of Grass	22
5	The Avenue of Standing Stones	27
6	Wanted: Dead or Alive	31
7	The Emperor of the De Danann Isle	36
8	Shapes of Mist and Shadow	41
9	The Dungeons of Falias	46
10	Earthmagic	52
11	Windmagic	57
12	Return to Falias	62
13	Diancecht the Healer	67
14	An Audience with the Emperor	72
15	The Healer's Promise	76
16	The Healer's Reward	82
17	In the Cage	86
18	The Earthlord's Tale	91
19	Earthmagic Again	96
20	The White Nathair	101
21	The Forest of Caesir	106
22	Scathach's Attack	111
23	The Gor Allta	116
24	Balor's Plan	121
25	The Red Stain	125
26	The King of the Isle	128
27	In the Tunnels	134
28	Scathach's Rescue	139
29	The Fomor Dungeons	144
30	The Stone Face	149
31	Across the Abyss	153
32	The Nathair Nests	158
33	Escape	164
34	The Earthlord	168

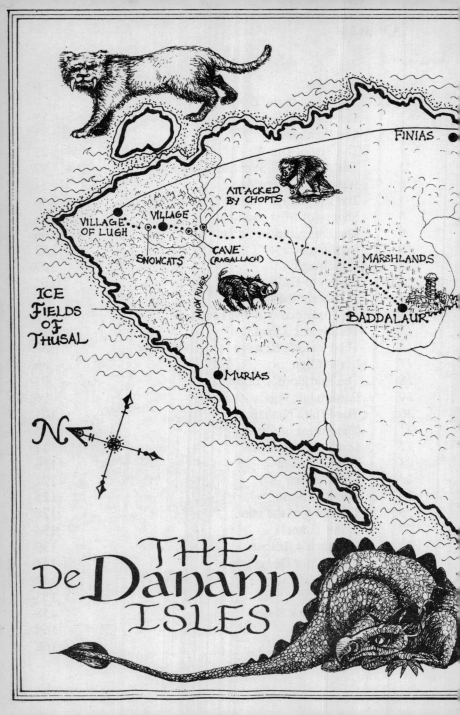

FINIAS

ATTACKED
BY CHOPTS

VILLAGE
OF LUGH

VILLAGE

SNOWCATS

CAVE
(RAGALLACH)

MARSHLANDS

ICE
FIELDS
OF
THUSAL

MUCK RIVER

BADDALAUR

N

MURIAS

THE
De Danann
ISLES

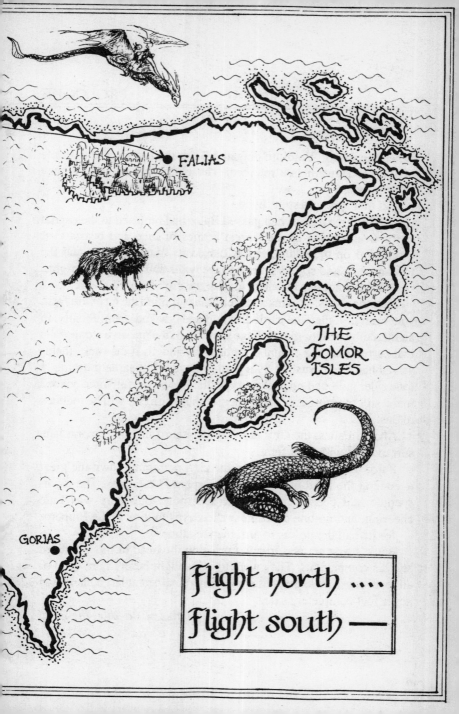

FALIAS

THE
FOMOR
ISLES

GORIAS

Flight north ....
Flight south —

When the young Windlord defeated Balor the Emperor, the people of the De Danann Isle rejoiced. The evil lord had finally been overthrown.

But their joy was short lived.

Before three moons had passed Balor had returned to the capital at the head of one of the largest armies of men and beasts ever assembled on the island. Falias closed its massive gates and the townspeople and soldiers manned the walls and prepared to fight.

Balor did not use his army to take the city; he used magic.

First the rivers, streams and wells that supplied the city with fresh water ran dry, then the earth dried up and cracked open. Finally, in an incredible feat of magic, huge sections of the massive stone walls that surrounded the capital crumbled to sand, as if the rocks themselves had been crushed by a giant's hand. That same morning, a lone rider galloped up to the city walls. His powerful voice echoed in the still morning air. 'Surrender, or the entire city will be reduced to dust.'

And so Falias, the City of Gold, capital of the De Danann Isle, surrendered without a fight.

Balor returned in triumph to the city, marching down the great avenue at the head of his army of serpent-like Fomor. The townspeople had been forced to line the route, but there was little cheering, and no-one dared raise their eyes to look at the Emperor — for he had the power to turn men to stone.

Balor's first act was to put a price on the head of the Windlord and his companions. They were to be brought before him, dead or alive, because he knew that while they remained at large, he would never feel completely safe.

Tales of Paedur, the Bard

white carpet. The weather forecasters had been promising snow for days, but Ken hadn't believed them. Maybe it would snow all night ... and then he stopped, suddenly realising that his parents would have to drive home through the snow-covered streets. He was turning away from the glass doors when he spotted movement at the bottom of the garden.

The Fomor felt the first icy kiss of a snowflake and winced with its sting. He turned his massive head to look up into the night sky. Snowflakes touched his scaly flesh, one melting against his flickering tongue. The beast spat out the the water droplet which tasted of smoke and metal. The Fomor was suddenly terrified. His kind were cold-blooded; the bitter cold could send him into a deep sleep, and then he would never be able to return to his own time.

More snowflakes stung his scales. He realised he would have to move in now!

It was probably nothing more than a cat or a dog at the bottom of the garden, Ken decided. But he remained standing at the glass doors, squinting out into the blackness. His breath misted on the glass and he ran his hand around in a small circle to look out.

He spotted movement again, a shadow flickering behind a bush. A big bulky shadow, man-sized.

A burglar?

Ken felt his heart begin to pound. He should go and warn Ally, but he couldn't move, he could only stare at the dark clump of shadow behind the bush. As he watched, the thickly falling snowflakes coated the figure, giving it a ghostly outline.

It was a man!

The house was locked up, the doors bolted, the windows closed. There was no way a burglar could get into the house, Ken reasoned, taking deep breaths, attempting to stay calm. He wiped the window clean again. He wished his parents had got a babysitter, but when they had suggested it, both he and his sister had argued that they were old enough to look after themselves; after all, Ally would be fifteen next birthday, and Ken was almost fourteen.

The glass had misted over again, and Ken ran his hand down it, wiping his wet palm on his jeans. The shadow by the bush was gone.

Ken breathed a huge sigh of relief: it had probably been nothing more than snow falling off the bush. He was surprised to find that his hands were trembling, and he felt a little ashamed at how easily he had been frightened. He was glad he hadn't run to tell Ally; she would never have let him forget it.

Ken pressed his face up against the cold damp glass, peering out into the garden for a final time ... and a monster's face appeared before him!

It was the face of a reptile, a long snout, flat, yellow, slit-pupilled eyes, a flickering tongue. Its jaws gaped, revealing long jagged teeth.

The boy jerked away from the window, crashing into the kitchen table, stumbling across a chair as he attempted to get out of the room.

Ally inched the tiny character on the screen forward to the edge of the river and then stabbed the fire button on the joystick. The tiny warrior leapt high into the air, landed on the rock in the middle of the river, bounced, bounced and bounced again, using the stones as a bridge. When she got him to the far side of the river, she sat back with a sigh, and wiped her sweating palm against her sleeve. She had never got this far in the game before. This was level three, the most dangerous level, filled with traps and monsters.

On screen the bushes parted and a two-headed dragon appeared, spitting fire....

'Fomor!' Ken crashed into the room, his scream startling her. Her hand jerked and her character jumped straight into one of the dragon's fireballs.

GAME OVER

'Ken!' Ally snapped, 'look what you've made me do ....'

'Fomor, Ally, Fomor!' Ken's voice had dropped to a hoarse, panicked whisper.

Ally swung around in the chair ... and then stopped when she saw the look of stark terror on her brother's face. 'What's wrong?' she demanded, coming to her feet. 'What's wrong?'

'F-F-f-Fomor,' he whispered. 'Downstairs.'

Ally smiled. 'Ken, don't be ridiculous....'

'I saw it,' he insisted.

Ally started to shake her head. She usually knew when her brother was playing a trick, trying to scare her. She'd be able to tell by the mischievous glint in his eye. But his eyes were wide and terrified. She shook her head. 'It can't be a Fomor,' she said.

'It's in the back garden,' her brother panted. 'I saw it hiding behind the bushes first. When I looked again, it had come right up to the back door.'

'It was probably nothing more than your own reflection. Or maybe the TV was reflecting something onto the glass.'

'It wasn't,' Ken said firmly, her disbelief turning his fear to anger. 'There was something there,' he insisted.

'Something? I thought you said it was a Fomor?' Ally said triumphantly.

'It was.'

Ally turned and marched out of the room.

'Where are you going?'

'I'm going to have a look.'

'Ally ... don't,' Ken shouted, but it was too late. His sister was at the bottom of the stairs. Taking a deep breath Ken raced downstairs after her.

Ally strode into the kitchen and turned on the lights. The fluorescent strips flickered and came alight. She walked right up to the sliding doors and peered out into the night. But all she could see was her own reflection in the glass. 'I can't see anything,' she said, 'turn off the lights.'

'Ally...' Ken began.

'Just turn them off,' she snapped.

Without taking his eyes off the doors, Ken hit the light switch with the palm of his hand, plunging the room into darkness.

Ally squinted out into the garden. Her eyes still hadn't fully adjusted to the darkness and she couldn't make out much. 'It's snowing,' she said in surprise.

'I know.'

'Well then, that's what you saw,' Ally said finally, turning away from the door. 'It was nothing more than the falling snow. Your imagination made it look as if....'

She stopped. Her brother was pointing towards the glass doors, mouth and eyes wide with terror.

Ally turned.

And looked into the snarling face of a Fomor warrior!

Paedur the Bard had been leaning across the fruit stall when he noticed the first of the black-clad troops beginning to file into the market square. Pulling the hood of his stained cloak higher over his head, he paid for the fruit with a copper coin and casually wandered over to the well in the centre of the square where Megan, the warrior maid, was filling two leather water skins.

'Trouble,' he muttered, not looking at her.

'I know.'

'It might just be a routine check,' Paedur murmured, rubbing a fat grape on his chest before popping it into his mouth.

'There are too many of them, and they're too well armed,' Megan said, straightening up, brushing strands of her brown hair out of her eyes. She reached under the loose fitting woollen robe she wore over her leather leggings and jerkin, making sure she could get to her blowpipe.

'If we get split up, I'll meet you at the lightning-struck tree on the outskirts of town,' Paedur murmured. His thin lips twisted into a smile. 'I thought we might have had a few days rest before they caught up with us.'

Megan returned his smile. 'The Emperor wants you very badly.'

'He wants you too,' the bard reminded her. 'Your name is on the wanted posters also.'

'But your name is in bigger print than mine,' she added. She tossed the two water skins across her shoulder and the young couple walked slowly across the square, dodging through the stalls selling fruits, vegetables, wooden implements, pots, pans, leather jerkins, cloaks, boots: everything a small frontier town would need. The bard paused at a stall selling wooden toys. He picked one up and pretended to look at it while quickly glancing behind to see what was happening. The soldiers were sealing off the entrances to the square.

A large hairy hand suddenly caught the front of his cloak, half-pulling him across the table. Paedur blinked in surprise as the huge wild-haired stall-keeper shook him. 'You wouldn't be stealing one of my little toys, now would you?'

'I would not,' Paedur said indignantly.

'Then where's your other hand?' the red-faced stall-keeper demanded. 'Got something hidden in it, eh?' He jerked back the bard's cloak, revealing the left arm which Paedur had kept hidden since they had entered the town. There was no hand on the end of the arm, only a shining silver half moon.

The stall-keeper's mouth opened in surprise, suddenly realising who the one-handed boy was ... suddenly remembering the huge reward.

'You're Paedur the Bard,' he gasped. Throwing back his head, he bellowed, 'The bard. It's the bard.'

Paedur's hook flashed upwards, the razor sharp edge slicing through the stall-keeper's beard, cutting it off. The toymaker dropped the boy with a terrified roar.

A soldier came around the corner of the stall, wondering what all the commotion was about. He spotted the one-handed boy and immediately dragged his sword free.

'Stop!' he shouted, and then grunted as Megan stepped up behind him and hit him on the back with the full water-skin. The leather sack exploded, the force of the unexpected blow and the weight of the water propelling the soldier into a fruit stall. The wooden table collapsed beneath his weight, fruit and vegetables cascading in around him.

Paedur and Megan raced across the square towards a narrow alleyway. They darted into it, wrinkling their noses at the stench of rotten fruit which had been dumped in the corners. A warrior appeared at the other end of the alleyway, a long spear held before him.

'Keep going,' Megan hissed. Reaching in under her robe, she pulled out her blowpipe, and then plucked a feathered dart from the pouch on her belt. Fitting the dart into the tube even as she ran, she waited until the warrior had reached the middle of the alley before she spat the dart at him.

Paedur, who was a few steps ahead of the girl heard the merest whisper as the dart buzzed past his ear. He saw the soldier ahead stop as if he'd run into an invisible wall. The man raised a hand and touched his neck and then he slowly sank to his knees. As Paedur and Megan raced past him, he was snoring gently, still on his knees.

They stopped at the end of the alley, Paedur peering to the left, Megan to the right. The coast was clear. Twenty steps ahead of them were the town walls. An old tumbled cottage had been built right up against the wall, its twisted chimney coming almost on a level with the top.

Paedur silently pointed to the rain barrel alongside the cottage, then to the roof, the chimney and then the wall. Megan nodded in understanding. She pulled the loose robe over her head. It had been a useful disguise to get into the town, but she didn't want it hampering her now.

'Go!' Paedur hissed.

Megan darted out of the alley, her soft-soled leather boots making no sound on the ground. She raced towards the cottage and jumped up onto the rain barrel. Catching the edge of the turf roof, she hauled herself upwards and then quickly shinned up the chimney and stepped onto the wall.

Paedur stepped out of the alley — just as four black-clad soldiers rounded the corner to his right. It took them a moment to react; then one man turned and ran back down the street, shouting for assistance, while the remaining three lifted their heavy crossbows and fired. The bard reached the rain barrel just as the first shot sped into the wood below his heel. Dirty water spouted out, puddling on the ground. The second crossbow bolt hissed into the turf roof above the bard's head. Paedur immediately caught his hook on the quivering bolt and used it to haul himself upwards. The third shot shattered off the chimney.

Paedur paused to wave back at the three soldiers who were struggling to reload before he dropped out over the other side of the wall.

By the time the guards reached the top of the wall, Paedur and Megan had vanished into the vast expanse of man-high grass.

Colman, the Captain of the Guard glared at the three crossbowmen. 'You had them in your sights and you let them go.' He swung around to look at the fourth man who had been found unconscious in the alleyway that led out onto the wall. The man was still groggy from the sleeping dart the girl had fired into his neck. 'And you allowed a boy and girl to walk past you!'

'They fired a dart at me,' the man protested.

Colman turned away in disgust. He climbed onto the top of the wall and looked out over the sea of tall waving golden grass. In places it was twice the height of a tall man, and while there were tracks and pathways cut through the Grasslands, finding someone in it would be impossible. The tall, broad-shouldered man ran his fingers through his greying beard. He didn't want to think about what would happen when the Emperor discovered that he had lost the bard and the girl. The girl was of little importance, but the two most wanted criminals in the De Danann Isle were the one-handed bard and the golden-haired Windlord. The Emperor wasn't going to be pleased ... and those who displeased the Emperor ended up being turned to stone.

Colman stepped off the wall and then dropped from the roof of the cottage onto the ground. 'Bring the birds,' he said wearily. 'If we cannot bring them back alive, then we will bring their bodies.'

'Slow down Megan. They'll never catch us now.' Paedur stopped and bent double, clutching at the stitch in his side. 'You can certainly run,' he said.

The brown haired, brown-eyed warrior maid trotted back to the bard, moving easily through the broad blades of grass that soared over their heads. 'Where I come from,' she said, 'if you can't catch your prey, you go hungry.' Megan came from one of the ice-locked villages close to the Top of the World. The bard wasn't sure how old she was — fifteen summers, he guessed — but she was fast and tough and a deadly shot with the blowpipe she carried. She had saved the lives of the bard and his companions on more than one occasion.

The girl stopped in front of Paedur, looking at the tall, dark-haired, dark-eyed youth, her gaze lingering on the curved half moon of metal that took the place of his left hand. She found herself wondering how he had lost his hand.

Paedur straightened. 'Going into the village was a mistake.'

Megan nodded. 'I did say that.'

'You were right. Now, the Emperor's men know where we are, we still have no food and no drinking water, and now we have no money.'

'I can find us food and water,' Megan said confidently. 'But what do we do now? Where are we going?'

'When the Fomor raided Baddalaur, I managed to get a message to Faolan to meet us at the Avenue of Standing Stones, on the eastern coast on the first night of the new moon. That's three nights from now.'

'How far are we from the place?'

'About three days, if we push hard...' Paedur began, and then he stopped, his head tilted to one side, listening.

'What is it?' Megan asked, her voice dropping to a whisper.

Paedur shook his head. 'The wind ... something....' He suddenly turned and pointed. High overhead the afternoon sun burned and winked off three objects high in the sky.

'What are they?' Megan asked, reaching into her pouch for a dart, sliding it into her blowpipe. 'They look like birds.'

Paedur started to shake his head. Suddenly the three birds folded their wings and dropped through the sky. When they were directly above Paedur and Megan, their wings snapped open, almost stopping them in mid air. Their shadows blotted out the sun, and suddenly Megan realised just how big the birds were.

'Giant eagles,' she whispered.

Paedur shook his head. 'Worse. Much worse, they're Iolar, hunting Iolar.' He pointed to the metal spurs on the birds' claws, the metallic sheen to their beaks, the spikes on the edges of their wings.

'What do they hunt?' Megan asked. The birds were close enough now for her to see their bright yellow eyes.

'Right now, they're hunting us!' he called.

Spreading their wings wide, their claws open, the birds dropped onto the couple.

The huge stone sword struck the sliding patio doors. The sheet of glass shattered with a thunderous explosion, spraying fragments across the room. Swinging the sword before him, the Fomor ducked through the frame, strode into the kitchen, his claws tearing through the lino floor covering. He couldn't allow them to escape. Batting a kitchen table aside, he strode after the humans, moving warily through the unfamiliar dwelling. There was a box in the corner of the next room: magical, twisting shapes moving across it, tiny humans trapped within the glass. One of the creatures drew a sword and advanced toward the beast. The Fomor's sword hacked through the television set, destroying it in an explosion of sparks and thick black smoke. The smoke curled and coiled around the fire alarm above the television, setting it off, the sudden ear-shattering whine terrifying the beast. He slashed at the circular white box with his stone sword, cutting a great gash in the ceiling as he chopped through it. The whine died to a squalk. Satisfied that he had slain the little demon, the Fomor went in search of the humans.

Ken and Ally struggled to push the wardrobe across the door to her room. 'This isn't going to stop it,' Ken stuttered. His teeth were chattering so badly he could barely speak.

Ally nodded. She had been terrified when she had seen the beast in the garden. But now that fear had turned to anger as she heard the Fomor smash through the house downstairs. She heard the smoke alarm scream briefly and suddenly wondered if the creature had set the house on fire.

'Ally, it's on the stairs,' Ken whispered, hearing the third stair from the bottom creak beneath the Fomor's weight. 'What are we going to do?'

Ally shook her head. She pressed both hands against the side of her face and closed her eyes, breathing deeply, attempting to think calmly and clearly. But this was a nightmare: a creature from thousands of years in the past had come through time in search of them. But why? When they had left the De Danann Isle six months ago, the Fomor and the Emperor had been defeated. Someone must have sent it forward through time, in the same way that Faolan the Windlord had sent them back to their own time.

'The pendants,' she said suddenly.

Ken looked at her blankly.

'The pendants Faolan gave us.'

Before they had left the De Danann Isle, Faolan had given each of them a small circular amulet which he'd created from the wind and air.

'He said if we ever needed him...' Ally said slowly.

'Or if we ever wanted to go adventuring again,' Ken added.

'Then all we had to do was hold them in our hands and breathe on them,' Ally finished. She ran across to her dressing table and pulled open her jewellery box. The silver pendant with the swirling cloud design was lying at the bottom of the box beneath a clutter of bracelets and bangles. She plucked it out, holding it tightly in her hand. 'Where's yours?' she asked.

'In my room,' Ken said quietly. Ken's room was at the other end of the landing.

The door to the room next to Ally's slammed open and they heard the beast moving through the room — their parents' room — pulling open wardrobe doors. Glass shattered.

'You go,' Ken said quickly. 'Breathe on the pendant — and go!'

'Don't be ridiculous.' She looked at the small metallic-grey object in the palm of her hand. She had seen the Windlord shape it out of a cloud, creating it with his magic. 'Maybe it could carry us both away,' she suggested.

Ken shook his head. 'If one had been enough, why give us two?'

The bedroom door suddenly shuddered, the wardrobe inching away from the door with the force of the blow.

'Do you know where yours is?' Ally demanded.

'Beside my Swiss Army Knife on the bookshelf over my bed.'

Another blow jerked the door back further. Ken pressed his back to the wardrobe, shoving it up against the door, but the beast was strong.

Ally ran to the window and pushed it open. It was snowing heavily now, huge silent flakes covering everything in a layer of white. Stray flakes whirled into the room. Directly across from her window, so close that the branches tapped against her glass when the wind blew, was a one hundred-year-old oak tree. Ken had often climbed up from the ground and sat in the branches of the tree, but it was a long time since she had tried it herself.

Ken screamed aloud as a massive sword blade snapped through the wardrobe inches from his head. The beast had driven its sword through the door and straight through the wardrobe. There was a ripping, cracking sound as the sword was pulled free.

'This way, Ken,' Ally shouted, puling back the window as far as it would go. Climbing onto the window ledge, she leaned out and touched the branches, now cold and wet with snow. Taking a deep breath, determined not to look down, she made a leap for the thickest branch. Twigs caught in her bright red hair, scratched her face and hands as she fell, and then all the breath was driven out of her as she landed across a branch. Coloured spots danced before her eyes. Stiff and bruised, she crawled along the branch to the trunk of the tree, wondering where her brother was.

Another blow hacked away a corner of the wardrobe, and then the stone sword punctured the wood twice in quick succession, gouging out an enormous hole. Ken leapt away from the wardrobe, jumping up onto the windowledge just as the Fomor smashed through the remains of the wardrobe. He strode into the room hissing in triumph as he spotted the boy.

Ken perched on the windowledge. He was so frightened he could barely feel his fingers, and he wasn't sure if his trembling legs would hold him.

The Fomor lashed out with the sword ... just as Ken jumped onto the tree. The stone blade sliced through the curtains, striking off the double-glazed glass, shattering it in a massive explosion of sound. Sparkles of glass rained down onto the snow covered garden.

Ken fell into the tree, crying out as a branch tore his arm and a twig scratched his face. He reached for a snow-covered branch, his hand slipping as he grabbed it, and then Ally's hand was gripping his wrist and she was hauling him upwards into the safety of the tree.

The branches and leaves before them suddenly disintegrated as the beast leaned out through the shattered remains of the window and slashed at them with his sword.

'Let's go,' Ally said tiredly. Ken followed her without a word. Ally slid down the tree trunk, skinning her hands on the rough bark. She waited until Ken had joined her at the bottom.

'Now what?' he demanded.

'Now we've got to get back into the house,' she whispered.

'What!'

'We need to get your pendant.'

'I'm not going back in there,' Ken whispered.

Above their heads, the Fomor squeezed through the space where the window had been and leapt into the tree. Twigs and broken branches rained down on the brother and sister. Without a word, they turned and ran around the side of the house, then darted through the broken patio doors into the kitchen, glass crunching beneath their feet. In the dining room, the wreck of the television set smouldered in the corner, the remains of the smoke alarm dangling from the torn ceiling. They both stopped, looking at the damage, wondering what their parents would say. Wood snapped in the garden, and they raced into the hall. The stairs had buckled and bowed beneath the creature's weight, some of them creaking alarmingly as Ally and Ken raced up them. When they reached the landing they discovered that the door to Ally's room lay in two shattered halves, slivers and chips of wood scattered everywhere.

In the kitchen below, glass shattered as the Fomor followed them back into the house. The beast crashed through the sitting room and out into the hall. For a single moment the two humans and the Fomor stared at one another ... and then Ken and Ally darted into Ken's bedroom.

Ally snapped the lock shut while Ken jumped onto the bed, scattering books from the shelves as he hunted desperately for the silver pendant.

The beast punched through the flimsy wooden door, its scaled claws ripping out a panel. Ally screamed and threw herself across the room away from the door. A second blow tore off the top hinge and the door tilted to one side. The Fomor caught the door in its claw and ripped it off its second hinge, tossing it back onto the landing behind it. Then, clutching its huge stone sword in both hands, it strode into the room.

Ken found his Swiss Army Knife. The pendant had been with it. But it wasn't there now.

The Fomor stopped. There was a box on the table to its right. Images were moving in the box, tiny humans and Fomor-like beasts fighting with swords and spears. As it watched a human threw a fireball at the tiny Fomor destroying it in a ball of flame.

Ken's fingers closed around the pendant; it had fallen down behind his books. Gripping it tightly in his left hand, he dived across the bed to where his sister was backed into a corner.

The Fomor struggled to make sense of what it was seeing. In the box, the tiny human killed another beast with a fireball. He knew this was a vile world; why, even the air and water tasted bad. He already knew that these humans were evil. And in the little box, he guessed, they kept the souls of dead or captured Fomor. No wonder the Emperor wanted them dead!

The beast lashed out with its sword, the point of the weapon punching through the computer screen, coming through the far side of the box in a shower of sparks.

The Fomor then turned its attention to the humans. They had led him a merry dance, but he had them now. The Emperor would reward him for this. Raising his sword high, he brought it swinging down in a great two-handed cut.

The bard shot out his left arm and the largest of the massive birds wrapped its metallic claws around his hook. Metal screamed off metal, bright yellow sparks dancing from the hook, singeing the bird's golden-brown feathers. The Iolar screamed with surprise and flapped upwards, the downdraft from its wings flattening the grass around the bard.

Megan managed to fire two darts in quick succession into the bird that swooped at her. She saw the creature's eyes glaze over and then close as the sleeping-honey which coated the darts took effect. But as the huge bird fell out of the sky, it crushed the young warrior maid to the ground, sending her blow-pipe spinning into the grass.

The third Iolar had circled around behind the couple before it swooped in low, its massive wings touching the top of the grass. The rustling alerted Paedur and he turned, but too late. The Iolar's metal-tipped claws bit into the bard's cloak, catching in the dusty material, dragging him up on his toes as the bird's wings beat in an effort to lift him into the sky. Paedur's hook flashed, cutting away a long piece of material. The sudden release caught the bird by surprise, and it went spiralling upwards. Paedur dropped heavily to the ground. Rolling over, he came stiffly to his feet; his back was a mass of bruises. He squinted up into the pale blue sky. The two Iolar were circling around them. Caught by surprise once, they would be far more dangerous the second time.

Megan slid out from beneath the sleeping bird. Crawling around on hands and knees, she patted the grass, looking for her blowpipe. Her fingers finally touched the thin wooden pipe. 'Got it.' Shading her eyes, she looked up at the birds. 'They're too far away for me to hit them. But if they get closer...' she added.

Paedur caught her arm and dragged her through the long grass. 'I don't think they'll try attacking us again,' he said, gritting his teeth as his bruised muscles protested. 'They'll simply circle overhead, marking our position, leading the Emperor's warriors directly to us.'

Megan glanced up into the sky again. 'If only we had some way of knocking them down.' She stopped suddenly, her brown eyes sparkling. 'Or hiding ourselves from them.'

The bard stopped and held up his hand. He tilted his head to one side, listening.

'What is it?' Megan asked.

'Listen,' Paedur whispered.

Faint in the distance, Megan heard the rough baying of hounds. She knew the type: mastiffs. Enormous dogs, incredibly strong and capable of following a scent for days. The warrior maid licked her index finger and held it up, testing the direction of the breeze. It was coming from behind her, blowing back towards the town, carrying her scent to the dogs. But she could use the wind to carry more than a scent. 'Fire,' she said simply.

Paedur looked at her for a moment, and then he nodded in understanding. 'Fire,' he agreed.

Colman, the Captain of the Guard, watched as the handlers brought out ten of the massive dogs. They were part dog, part wolf, each one wearing spiked leather armour, spiked collars and had leather masks protecting the delicate bones of their faces. Once they picked up a scent they would follow it to the ends of the earth.

Colman shaded his eyes and squinted up into the heavens. He could see two of the Iolar circling over a spot off to the north. He wondered what had happened to the third eagle; had they managed to slay it, and how?

One of his black-clad troop stopped in front of him and saluted. There was a ragged cloak in his hand. 'The girl was seen to drop this before the couple made their escape over the walls.'

Colman snatched it from his grasp. 'Excellent. Give it to the dogs. Its scent will lead them directly to the girl at least.'

'If the dogs catch them, they will tear the couple apart.'

'The Emperor wants them dead or alive. He would prefer to have them alive ... but only so that he can have the pleasure of slaying them himself. But don't take any chances with them. They are both extremely dangerous. If the dogs get to them first, just bring me back their heads!'

Paedur's hook rang off a flat sliver of flint. Sparks fell to the piece of oil-dampened cloth Megan held in her hands. One of the sparks hissed on the damp cloth, then popped alight. Holding the cloth by one end, Megan quickly whirled it around, fanning the flame to a blaze. When the cloth was burning strongly, she carefully dragged it across the base of the walls of grass. The thick green and brown stems smouldered, smoked, turned black and then crackled as flames took hold. A thin thread of grey-white smoke spiralled upwards, disturbing the Iolar's circling. The smoke thickened, then darkened as flames began to race up the length of the grass, fanning out of either side. Within moments, the wind was blowing a wall of flame, higher than a man, away from the young couple, back towards the town. Plumes of dark grey-black smoke darkened the sky, driving the Iolar away, blotting out the sun.

'Let's go.' Paedur turned and ran through the sea of grass, following an almost invisible animal trail. Megan followed, moving silently through the long grasses.

When they paused for breath in a small clearing, she turned and looked back. The sky had darkened, thick clouds twisting and curling upwards. Flames were leaping high and the air was filled with burning cinders which, as they fell, set other portions of the grass fields alight. 'What have we done?' she asked in a horrified whisper. 'I never thought....'

'Don't worry,' Paedur said quietly. 'Every season, the townspeople set the Sea of Grass alight. They gather at one end and catch the countless creatures that are fleeing from the flames. When the fires die down, they will clear as much as they can and plant vegetables in the rich soil. They would hope to get in at least one harvest before the grass reclaims the cleared areas.' He slashed at the grass with his hook. 'If they didn't cut and burn the grass, it would soon take over the entire De Danann Isle.'

'Where to now?' Megan asked.

'We'll make for the Avenue of Standing Stones. And let's hope Faolan and Ragallach are there.'

In a dungeon beneath the Emperor's palace in Falias, the Capital of the South, Balor stood beside a young dark-haired dark-skinned boy. Spread out on the floor of the dungeon was a perfect map of the entire De Danann Isles, from the Ice fields of Thusal in the North to the Fomor Isles in the far South. Burning torches set high on the walls cast flickering shadows across the map, making it seem as if the rivers were flowing, or that the wind was blowing through the trees in the Forest of Caesir.

The Emperor rested his human hand on the boys shoulder. He held a long stone Fomor sword in his left hand and he used it to point to a tiny model of a city in the bottom left hand corner of the map. 'The people of Gorias have not accepted me as their ruler,' Balor said softly, touching the model with the tip of his long sword. 'When the cursed Windlord used his magic to drive me from this city, the people of Gorias, like many of the people of the De Danann Isle, assumed that I was gone forever. And now that I have returned, they have refused to accept my rule. They have imprisoned my messengers, attacked my troops, insulted me. I think it is time to send them a message they will not be able to ignore.' The Emperor's grip tightened on the boy's shoulder. 'Destroy the city for me.'

The boy shook his head. 'I will not.'

'Oh yes you will, Colum,' Balor said very quietly. His grip tightened and the boy winced in pain. 'Never forget: I have your mother, brother and sister safe in the caves on the Fomor Isles. Their well-being depends upon your co-operation.'

Colum nodded slowly. 'What do you want me to do?' he asked eventually.

Balor rammed his sword through the model of Gorias, destroying it. 'Since your father's death you are the Earthlord. You control the elemental magic of this island, the force that flows through the soil. Use your magic now to tear the town apart.'

Colum nodded wearily. Pulling off his boots, he felt the cold stone beneath his feet. Stretching out his hands, he touched the walls of the dungeon on either side. Closing his eyes, he allowed the ancient earth magic, the magic of the soil, the same magic that had built mountains, caved valleys, shaped hills and caves, to flow into his body. He became aware of the De Danann Isle as if it were a living organism, from the chill of the Northlands to the sweltering heat of the Western Deserts. Smoke coiled around his nostrils and he coughed suddenly, tasting burnt grass on the air, feeling the pain of burned earth beneath his feet.

'What is wrong?' Balor demanded.

'Fire,' Colum breathed. 'Fire in the Sea of Grass.'

The Emperor automatically looked at the spot on the map, and his single eye narrowed. The bard and the warrior maid had been sighted close to one of the towns that bordered the vast area of tall, fast-growing grasses.

'Ignore it,' Balor hissed. 'Destroy Gorias.'

Calling up the earth magic, the young Earthlord visualised a long ragged tear parting the ground upon which the city was built.

On the far side of the De Danann Isle, an earthquake devastated Gorias, the City of Iron, tumbling houses and palaces, shattering the thick walls that surrounded the city. Even while the earth tremors were still shaking the city, an army of the Emperor's Fomor troops marched through the city's broken walls.

Gorias surrendered without a fight.

The huge stone sword swept down, slicing through the bookshelf over Ken and Ally's head....

Ken and Ally vanished

...the point of the stone biting deeply into the wooden floor, throwing the Fomor off balance. The beast reached out with a trembling claw, waving it in the air where, moments before, the two humans had cowered. The creature's forked tongue flickered, tasting the air, sorting through the countless scents in the bedroom. Most of the odours were strange and alien, but there was one familiar smell, a sharp, bitter scent. The metallic odour of De Danann magic.

The Fomor straightened and pulled his sword from the floorboards. The Emperor would not be pleased, and the Fomor felt a brief flicker of fear, wondering what would happen when he returned without the human-kind. But at least he knew now where the humans had gone; they had returned to the De Danann Isle.

Ally breathed on the pendant as the sword was falling, screaming as it cut through the air....

She felt her stomach lurch and a bitterly cold wind blasted into her face, making her squeeze her eyes shut. Ken's grip tightened on her hand, his nails biting deep into her flesh. She opened her mouth to scream, but the cold wind sucked the air from her lungs. It roared around her head, the howling gale lashing her hair across her face, blowing sand into her mouth.

Sand?

Ally opened her eyes as the wind died. She was lying face down beside her brother on a golden sanded beach.

Ken turned his head and opened one eye to look at her. 'I don't know where we are.'

'I don't care where we are; at least we're safe from the Fomor,' Ally said firmly. She ran the back of her hand across her lips, brushing away the grains of sand. 'The pendants worked,' she said, sitting up. 'We've been pulled back in time to the De Danann Isle.' She stood up and looked around.

They were lying at the bottom of an enormous sand dune. Twisted and tangled grass rasped drily along the top of the dune, while close-by, on the other side of the dune, they could hear the roar and hiss of the surf on the shore.

'We're on a beach,' Ken said, scrambling up the side of the sand dune, grabbing the grass on the top to help him up. He hissed in pain as the razor sharp blades cut into the soft flesh of his palm. Bright red spots of blood dripped onto the golden grains.

'It's marram grass,' Ally said, climbing slowly up the side of the dune, being careful not to touch the grass. 'Its roots help hold the dunes together.'

Ken patted the blood with a dirty hanky. 'They might be holding the roots together, but they very nearly cut my hand off at the same time.'

'It's only a scratch.' Standing on the top of the dune, she turned towards the sea, breathing deeply, filling her lungs with the cold damp sea air. The sea was a brilliant, almost hard blue, the foam of the breaking waves looking as if they had been painted onto a piece of glass. Shading her eyes, Ally looked up into the clear sky. The sun was almost directly overhead, and she guessed that it was close to noon.

Ken stood with his back to her, looking in the opposite direction. 'I wish I knew where we were,' he said.

'So do I,' Ally said, turning around. She stopped when she saw what her brother had been looking at.

Two long lines of standing stones stretched away from the beach on either side of the remains of what had once been an enormous smoothly paved road. The road was now overgrown, partially covered in sand, broken through in places by the thick grass. Following the line of the road, Ally could see where it ran straight down to the beach and out under the sea.

Ken scrambled down off the sand dune and onto the remains of the road. It was only when he was standing on it that he realised just how broad it was. It was easily as wide as a dual carriageway, and there were shallow grooves worn into the stone where chariots and carts had once run. 'I wonder how old it is,' he murmured. He stepped over to the nearest standing stone and ran his hand down the surface, brushing away a layer of dirt and sand to expose the bare rock. 'Look Ally, they've got carvings on them.' He traced a spiral with his index finger. 'They're just like the designs on the Newgrange Stones.'

Ally slid down the sand dune to stand beside her brother. She counted twelve stones on either side, each one almost twice her height. Two of the pillars had tumbled over and another two had snapped in half. 'There were probably pieces across the top,' she said, 'like Stonehenge.'

Ken shook his head. 'The tops are rounded,' he pointed out, 'not flat.'

Ally looked around. 'I wonder where the road went ... or came from.'

'From the capital, I shouldn't wonder,' Ken said, rubbing away more of the dust, tracing another pattern on the stone. The twisting spirals, circles and curls were definitely Celtic. The design was vaguely similar to the pendant which he now wore around his neck.

'Do you think if we follow this road we'll end up in Falias?' Ally asked. She pulled strands of red hair back off her face and fished in her pocket for an elastic band. While she was pulling her hair into a crude ponytail, she looked down along the length of the broken road. 'I wonder how far we are from the capital?'

'We don't even know if it goes to the capital. And anyway, I'm not sure we should go there,' Ken added, turning away from the stones, walking over to his sister.

'Why not?'

'Someone sent that Fomor forwards into our own time.'

'So?'

'That creature was going to kill us, Ally,' Ken said very softly, his voice suddenly beginning to tremble. He had just realised how close they had come to death. 'Only a very powerful magician would have been able to send the Fomor after us.'

'Balor?' Ally whispered. 'But Faolan defeated him.' She sat down on the stump of a pillar, her legs suddenly shaky.

Ken shook his head. 'That was six months ago; a lot could have happened in that time.'

'So what do we do? Do we stay here and hope someone comes along, or do we go in search of a village or town?'

Ken shrugged. He turned around in a complete circle, but there was no sign of buildings in any direction. 'We need to find out what has happened. We've got to try to find Paedur, Faolan and the others....' He stopped suddenly.

'What is it?' Ally came to her feet.

Ken pointed down the road. Through the shimmering heat haze he could make out two figures — one tall, one short — coming towards them.

The figures stopped ... and then they suddenly started running towards the two humans. Sunlight glinted off the metal tipped spears they carried.

'Run!' Ken shouted.

'Where?' Ally demanded.

A sudden roar startled the seabirds, sending them wheeling up into the sky. 'Ken ... Ken ... Ally ... Ally.'

'I know that voice...' Ally began. Shading her eyes with her hand, she squinted at the two figures. Her face broke into a broad smile. 'Ragallach,' she shouted, recognising the huge Torc Allta. The boar-like creature, with its great curling tusks and its thick reddish hair walked like a human during the hours of daylight, but at night it assumed the shape of a small pink pig. Even though he was not fully grown, Ragallach was enormous, incredibly strong, and terrifying looking. Ever since Ally had rescued him from a pit, they had become close friends.

The Torc Allta swept the girl up in his paws, easily lifting her off the ground, holding her without any effort.

She wrapped her hands around his enormous neck, smelling the slightly musty odour of his hair. 'Ragallach, it's good to see you again.'

The beast's thick lips moved, forming the words carefully. His pink eyes were wide in astonishment. 'What are you doing here? How did you get back?'

'I told you I smelt magic in the air,' Ragallach's companion said, hurrying up to join them.

'Faolan?' Ken asked uncertainly. 'Is that you?' He was looking at a boy of around his own age. Faolan was the Windlord. He could control the wind, the most powerful of the elemental magics. The last time he had seen Faolan, the boy had been dressed in the garments of a prince, but now Ken found himself looking at a small, scruffy vagabond, clad in torn rags, his golden hair hidden beneath a wide-brimmed hat. The boy tilted back the hat and Ken caught a glimpse of the Windlord's bright golden eyes. 'It *is* you!'

Faolan squeezed Ken's shoulder. 'Of course it's me — who else do you think would be travelling with this ugly creature.'

Ragallach put Ally down. 'You're not only ugly to me human-kind,' he said, his lips drawing back from his teeth in what Ally had learned was a smile, 'but you forget my senses are sharper than yours.' He winked at the human girl. 'And he smells.'

Faolan pulled off his hat and ran his hands through his hair. It was greasy and in need of a wash. 'It's good to see you both. Have you been here long?'

'A few moments,' Ally said. Lifting her right hand, she showed the Windlord the pendant. 'We had to use the presents you gave us, because....'

Faolan held up his hand. 'Wait. We both have tales to tell. Let's find a place to sit down and see if we can get something to eat. I don't know about you, but I'm starving.'

'You're always hungry, human,' Ragallach grumbled. He turned towards the beach. 'I'll see if I can catch us some fish.'

As the Torc Allta strode away, Ally turned to Faolan. 'What is this place?' she asked.

'The Avenue of Standing Stones,' Faolan said, looking around. 'This land is now called the Isle of the Tuatha De Danann, but before our people came to this place another, older race, ruled the island. We know very little about them, but all across the island and in the lands that border the island you can find the ruins of their cities and roads. They were a great race,' he added quietly, 'some say they were gods, or the sons of gods.' He shivered, even though it was the middle of the day. 'I can feel the magic in this place. Old magic. Powerful magic.'

'Evil magic?' Ken asked, looking at the stones again.

Faolan shook his head. 'There is no evil magic, only evil people.' There was a shout of triumph from the beach. Faolan forced a smile to his lips. 'Aaah, lunch I think.'

It tasted delicious. Ragallach had caught three enormous dark-skinned fish that looked like haddock, and they had cooked them on a driftwood and seaweed fire built on the smooth stones of the ancient road.

Ragallach sat with his back against one of the standing stones, carefully picking the flesh off the fishbones, listening to Ken and Ally's story about the Fomor that had come forward in time to kill them.

'I don't know what Mum and Dad are going to say when they get back and find the house completely wrecked,' Ally finished.

'What's been happening here?' Ken asked, looking from the Torc Allta to Faolan. 'When we left here Balor had been defeated, blown away by your wind magic, the Fomor were retreating to their island homes. What happened?'

Faolan wiped the back of his hand across his greasy mouth. Standing up, he looked out to sea, watching storm clouds gather on the horizon. 'Balor returned,' he said eventually.

Ragallach tossed the remains of his fish onto the fire, where it hissed, the fish oils feeding the flames. 'Start at the beginning, Faolan,' he said gently.

'You tell the tale,' the Windlord murmured.

The Torc Allta nodded. 'How much time has passed in your world?' he asked.

Ally shrugged. 'Six months ... six full moons.'

'Less than half that time has passed here. When you and Ken returned to your own time, we felt as if the adventure was at an end. Faolan and I joined Paedur at Baddalaur, the College of Bards. I began training as the first non-human bard in the history of the college, while Faolan began taking lessons in how to control and use his magic. Megan bid us farewell and headed off to the East in search of adventure.'

'What happened?' Ken said urgently.

Ragallach held up a huge paw. 'Be patient. Less than a moon had passed when we heard disturbing rumours out of the East. Earthquakes had shaken the land, destroying whole towns and villages. Rivers had sprung up where there had been none before, sleeping fire-mountains had spewed flames and rock into the air, whole mountains had crumbled, while new ones had risen in their place.'

'Powerful magic,' Faolan said quietly without turning around.

Ragallach nodded. 'There are four ancient lords of magic: the Windlords, the Firelords, the Sealords ... and the Earthlords. The

33

Master Bards in Baddalaur said that the Earthlords were calling upon their magic to rend and tear the land.'

'But why?' Ally whispered.

'Because they are in league with Balor,' Faolan said simply.

'It's true,' Ragallach agreed. 'The Master Bards could feel the energy being drawn from the entire De Danann Isle as the Earthlords worked their magic. A few days later, a messenger arrived from Balor. There was one demand: if we did not surrender, Balor would destroy Baddalaur first and then Falias.'

'What did you do?' Ally asked.

'We did nothing. But two days later, all the small villages around the College of Bards vanished into huge holes that opened up beneath them. Many died.'

'So you surrendered,' Ken said.

'There was nothing else we could do.'

'Megan returned,' Faolan said suddenly, taking up the story. He turned around and sat down, facing them. 'She had been in the East when the Emperor's attacks had started. She had seen at first hand what he had done, what power he commanded. And she had also learned that Balor had offered a huge reward for the capture of the people who had been responsible for his defeat.' He pulled a thick piece of folded paper from inside his torn jerkin. 'This has been posted up in every town and village across the Isle.

'*A thousand crowns for information leading to the capture of the one-handed bard, by name Paedur. The same reward for the youth Faolan, a petty magician, pretending to be the Windlord. Five hundred crowns for the Torc Allta, Ragallach; the same reward for the savage tribeswoman, Megan. Two hundred crowns for their red-haired companions.*'

'Originally the reward was offered for our capture alive,' Ragallach continued, 'but now it's dead or alive.'

'Where are Paedur and Megan now?' Ally asked.

'On their way here, I hope,' Faolan sighed. 'The Fomor raided Baddalaur shortly after Megan arrived. I don't know what happened to Megan, but I saw the bard briefly. He said that if we became separated, we would meet here, on the Avenue of Standing Stones on the first night of the new moon.'

'When is that?' Ken wondered.

'Tonight,' Ragallach smiled.

Ally shivered. 'Are we in danger?'

The huge Torc Allta shrugged. 'The most powerful magician in the known world and his army of reptilian Fomor are after us. We have a price on our heads that would satisfy a king. We have two spears, two knives, my strength during the day, Faolan's magic ... which we cannot use, because it would alert Balor to our position.' He nodded firmly. 'Yes, I'd say we're in trouble.'

Ally looked into the Torc Allta's pink eyes. 'We defeated the Emperor once before. We can do it again,' she said fiercely.

'He was unprepared the last time,' Ragallach reminded her. 'Now, he knows what he's up against.'

The girl smiled. 'He's already tried to kill us and capture you. And he's failed.'

'Ally's right,' Ken said. 'Maybe he's worried now.'

'Why would he be worried?' Faolan asked.

'Because what we did once before, we can do again. We can defeat him!'

'So what do you suggest we do?' the Windlord asked sceptically.

Ken grinned. 'We should do what he least expects us to do. Return to Falias; attack him there!'

'It's madness,' Faolan said, shaking his head quickly.

'On the contrary,' a new voice said, from the other side of the standing stone, 'it's brilliant.' As Ragallach surged to his feet with his spear in his hand, Paedur and Megan stepped out from behind the stone pillars.

Balor, the Emperor of the De Danann Isle, sat on his throne of polished black marble and listened as Colman, Captain of the Guard, stuttered out his story.

'They escaped across the Sea of Grass, my lord. We sent Iolar against them, but the cursed bard and the savage warrior maid defeated them. We were bringing up the hounds when they set fire to the grass. It took every man to control the blaze...' he finished lamely.

'So they got away,' Balor rumbled. He was dressed entirely in black, from his high black boots to his thick leather jerkin. The terrified captain could see himself reflected in the smooth silver metal mask that covered one half of the Emperor's face.

'My lord, they are demons.'

The Emperor ignored him. He raised his head slightly and the two Fomor guards at the other end of the room immediately opened the door. Two Fomor in full armour strode into the chamber, marched to the foot of the throne and immediately bowed deeply, their heads actually touching the top step.

'Stand,' Balor said. His long-fingered black-nailed hand slid across his mask, gently scratching the metal.

The two beasts stood. One was enormous, even amongst the Fomor, a huge ugly warrior, his flat reptilian features now scarred after a lifetime of war. He wore a metal eye-patch over his left eye. He was wearing the leather and metal armour of the Fomor warriors, and carried his huge stone sword in its sheath on his back. He was Cichal, Captain of the Fomor Guard, one of the few creatures the Emperor allowed to bear weapons in his presence.

The second Fomor was smaller — though he still towered over Colman — and his skin was green and gleaming. His forked tongue was flickering nervously and his spiked tail kept twitching.

Balor ignored Cichal and glared at the younger Fomor. 'Report,' he snapped.

'I am Goll, Warrior of the Fomor,' the creature began. He kept his head low, not meeting the Emperor's gaze.

'You are young, Goll?' Balor asked, interrupting him.

'Yes, lord,' the Fomor said, surprised.

The Emperor looked at Cichal. 'Why was this young warrior sent on such an important mission?'

Cichal raised his head and stared proudly at Balor. 'He is my hatchling, lord.'

'Your son?'

Cichal nodded. 'The human-kind would call him my son; he was hatched in my nest on the Fomor Isles.'

'Why did you allow your son to be sent forward along the Timewinds to the world of these red-haired human-kind? You knew it was a dangerous mission.'

'This band of humans, Paedur, Faolan, Megan, the Torc Allta and the red-haired humans humiliated me. It is only right and fitting that one of my own hatchlings should be the instrument of my vengeance, and so restore my honour.'

Balor nodded. Although his mother had been human, his father had been a Fomor officer and he had been raised on the Fomor Isles. He knew all about the Fomor code of honour. Turning back to Goll, he fixed him with his single green eye. 'Make your report then, Goll.'

'The Timewinds carried me to a place of demons, a place of stone forts, of metal beasts that swallow the human-kind, where globes of burning fire light even unused streets. Every street is paved with smooth stone, and there is glass everywhere: glass windows, glass doors, even glass walls.'

'A place of powerful magicians,' Balor said slowly.

'It was cold, lord. Snow covered everything, but within their stone forts the humans went with only the lightest of clothing. Globes and strips of white fire lit every chamber, slender metal boxes set onto the walls gave off heat. And there were other boxes, smaller, fatter, which showed images of trapped humans and beasts.' The beast's voice trembled, remembering the terrifying images.

'Make your report,' Cichal snapped.

The young Fomor bowed quickly. The images he had seen in the demon-world would stay with him to the end of his days. He still woke in the middle of the night, shouting aloud his fear.

'I made my way into the demon-fort. But the human-kind were ready for me. They barricaded themselves in one of the chambers. By the time I managed to break through, they had escaped through a window. When I cornered them a second time, they were both trapped in a small bed-chamber. I decided then lord, that I could not bring them back alive, so I resolved to take their heads.'

Balor nodded. 'Good thinking.'

'But they vanished.'

'Vanished?' The Emperor looked from Goll to Cichal. 'Vanished!'

'They were as close to me as this human....' Goll put his hand on Colman's shoulder. 'I brought my sword down ... and in that instant they vanished. My sword plunged into the floor. There was magic in the air, lord, I could taste it.' His tongue flickered automatically. 'It was De Danann magic, I'm convinced of it. It smelt exactly the same as the magic which sent me to that dreadful place.' Goll nodded quickly. 'Aye lord, they have returned here. The red-haired humans have returned to the De Danann Isle.'

Balor surged to his feet, sending Goll and Colman staggering backwards with fright. Cichal didn't move. The expression on the Emperor's face was terrifying. His pale greasy skin was dark with rage, his thin-lipped mouth twisted into an ugly sneer. He glared at the two officers, and for a single moment, they both thought he was going to remove the metal mask. If he did that, then they both knew they would be joining the hundreds of statues that lined the Great Hallway that led to this chamber. No-one alive had seen what lay beneath the Emperor's mask: the sight was so horrific that it turned men and beasts to stone.

'Dismissed,' Balor thundered. 'Not you Cichal,' he added.

The two officers bowed deeply and then scuttled backwards, their heads bent low. They were both surprised that they were still alive.

Balor snapped his fingers and the Fomor guards on either side of the door bowed and stepped outside, leaving the Emperor alone with Cichal.

The huge Fomor regarded the Emperor warily. Although he feared neither man nor beast, he was terrified of the Emperor. He had heard some Fomor say that they were not afraid of Balor ... but they were fools, and far too many of them ended up as pieces of frozen sculpture in the hall.

'So the red-haired human-kind have returned,' Balor said quietly, almost as if he were talking to himself. 'The bard and the warrior-maid have also escaped us, and we have not had a report of the Windlord and the Torc Allta since they slipped away from Baddalaur.' He strode across to the enormous circular window that took up most of one wall. The window was shaped like a huge eye. From the distance it seemed like a solid piece of glass, but it was actually made up of hundreds of small pieces welded together. From this window, Balor could look out over the entire city of Falias. 'We need to capture this band of renegades,' he continued.

'They are a nuisance, nothing more,' Cichal said cautiously.

'They mock me. Their very freedom mocks my laws. They make fools of my warriors. Soon, people will look to them and say "if they can do it, why can't I," and from there it is a short step to rebellion.' Balor turned around, standing with his back to the circle of glass, the early morning sunlight outlining him in harsh white light. Cichal blinked, his single yellow eye watering. 'If all the people of the De Danann Isle were to rise up against me tomorrow, could your Fomor troops and the human warriors stand against them?'

Cichal shook his head. 'We rule through fear lord, you know that. There is perhaps one warrior for every hundred citizens.'

Balor sighed and turned back to the window. The magnificent city of Falias, the city of gold, was spread out below him, a confusing jumble of streets and alleys, where both men and beasts mingled together, worked, traded, fought, married and died.

And they all hated him.

The idea brought a smile to his lips. Emperors didn't have to be loved; love was a sign of weakness, a sign of fear. A woman who loved her children was frightened for them, a boy who loved a girl was terrified that something might happen to her. Balor ruled by taking advantage of the humans' love for one another.

But now he too felt an emotion that was strange and frightening; he felt the whisper of fear. These renegades had defeated him once before; they could do that again. On the very steps of this palace they had turned his magic against him, sweeping him up in a ghost wind, tossing him to the other end of the De Danann Isle. A lesser man would have been destroyed, but he was no mere human, he was Balor, half human, half Fomor. And he had returned in triumph. He would not allow five humans and a were-beast to defeat him.

'If I increase the reward for the renegades, I will only make them more important than they already are,' he said suddenly.

Cichal nodded.

'I want you to pick ten of your best men ... I don't care if they are human, Fomor or even were-beast. Offer them a hundred thousand crowns apiece for every one of the band they bring back here. But I want at least one of them alive!'

'It would be easier to bring back their bodies,' Cichal said quickly.

'I know that. But if we can even capture just one of them, then the others will come in to the rescue.' He nodded quickly. 'Then we will have them. Take whatever you need to accomplish your mission.'

'Yes my lord.' Cichal bowed low and backed away from the Emperor. He had reached the door when Balor spoke again.

'And Cichal?'

'Yes, my lord.'

Balor turned from the window. One half of his face was in shadow, but the sunlight ran like liquid off his metal mask. 'You failed me once before Cichal, and I forgave you. I will not forgive you again.'

Seated around a snapping fire of foul-smelling seaweed and drift-wood, eating roasted fish and shellfish which Ragallach and Megan had found, the six companions made their plans.

Paedur and Megan had quickly told what had happened to them since they had fled Baddalaur: how they had been chased from town to town by the Emperor's troops, and how they had almost been caught in the town on the edge of the Sea of Grass.

'They will never stop,' he finished. He looked across at Ken. 'Your plan is good, but I have a suggestion....'

'What is that?' Faolan asked.

'The Emperor wants me,' Paedur said, his lips twisting in a smile, firelight and shadows dancing across his face. 'Possibly if he gets me, he will stop looking for you. He seems to think I am the ringleader of this bunch of renegades.'

'You are,' Faolan grinned. 'You're older and certainly wiser than any of us. Your bardic training has prepared you to command.'

Paedur nodded. 'So if I were to be sighted in the Ice Fields of Thusal, for example, that would mean the Emperor would send his men there.'

The four humans nodded. The Torc Allta, who had transformed into a pig shape as the sun's rays had finally disappeared, was lying on the ground at Ally's feet, its head on her leg. Its small pink eyes were shut and its snout was opening and closing as it breathed. Ally thought she could hear snores.

'How do you propose to do that?' Faolan asked finally.

Paedur shrugged. Leaning forward, he speared a ragged piece of wood with the point of his hook and tossed it onto the fire. Dozens of sparks spiralled upwards into the night sky. Sitting back into the shadows, he continued. 'You can use your wind-magic to send me.'

Ken looked up quickly. 'But I thought if you used any magic then that would attract the Emperor's attention?'

Megan nodded. She was sitting close to the fire, carefully cutting wood to make darts for her blow-pipe. 'Ken is right. You can be sure that the Emperor's magicians are carefully watching for any uses of magic, especially powerful elemental magic, like Faolan's.'

Paedur nodded quickly. 'I know that. But by the time the Emperor would be able to get Fomor here, we would be gone.'

Ally leaned forward, the firelight making her red hair look like metal threads. 'But I don't see the point,' she snapped. 'All we would be doing is wasting time. I agree with Ken: we should carry the fight to the Emperor. We should go to Falias and then...' she stopped.

'And then what?' Paedur asked quietly. 'I agree that Balor will not be expecting us to return to the capital. But once we reach Falias, what are we going to do? Before we even begin the journey, we should at least have a plan worked out.'

'Once we're in Falias, we can contact my parents,' Faolan said. 'With my mother, father and sister to help us with their wind magic, we will be able to blow away anything that stands in our way.'

'I'm just surprised they haven't done anything so far,' Paedur said quietly. He dropped a hand on Faolan's shoulder. 'Let's hope they're all right.'

'They'll be all right,' Faolan said confidently. 'They are the Windlords.'

Paedur attempted a smile. He wasn't as confident as Faolan.

'How close are we to the capital?' Ken asked.

'This place, the Avenue of Standing Stones is about two days' journey from the capital. We can follow the remains of the road straight into the Door of the Gods, which is the oldest gate in Falias.'

Faolan yawned. 'I suggest we sleep on it. It's been a long day — for all of us.' He turned and grinned at Ally and Ken. 'In fact, for you, it's been a couple of thousand years long!'

Paedur nodded. 'We'll talk about it in the morning then. We should post a guard,' he added. 'Not that I think there's any danger,' he added, seeing the look of alarm on Ally's face. 'However, I don't think we should take any risks. I'll take the first watch; Megan, will you take over from me?'

'What about the rest of us?' Faolan asked.

'Megan and I are used to it. Bards are trained to go for long periods without sleep, and Megan comes from a land where the days are often very short, and the nights equally long. She is used to snatching a few hours' sleep when she can. We've got a hard road ahead of us over the next two days, I want you all fit and rested.'

Ken made a face. 'It just doesn't seem fair.'

Paedur's smile was cold. 'This isn't a game, played by some rules, with a code of what is right and what is wrong. I told you before, if you are hurt or injured in this world, in this time, you will carry that injury back to your own time. If you are killed here....' He stopped and shrugged. 'So you see ... I cannot afford to take the risk with your lives, or with ours. Tonight, you will sleep,' Paedur said firmly. 'You'll get your chance to stay awake all night soon enough.' Leaning forward, he scattered the fire with his hook, tossing sand onto the flames.

'Are there any dangerous animals around here?' Ally asked, trying to make herself comfortable on the hard sand.

Paedur considered. 'Not many,' he answered finally.

And suddenly Ally wasn't so sure that she was going to get much sleep that night!

The ghosts came in the darkest part of the night, when the stars had faded and the sky had not yet begun to lighten. Ice-grey mist flowed silently off the standing stones like smoke, coiling and twisting in strange patterns that matched the designs cut into the stone. The mist grew thicker, flowing into twelve tall, vaguely human shapes. Shadows formed on the shapes, hinting at faces, deep dark shadowy eyes, another dark hole was a mouth, while long wispy strands of mist suggested hair.

The twelve ghosts drifted noiselessly towards the figure of the young bard.

Paedur was desperately tired. What he had said about bards being trained to stay awake was true, but he hadn't really slept properly since he and Megan had fled Baddalaur, four days previously. What he would give now for a warm, comfortable bed!

Paedur looked towards the sea. Although it was invisible in the night, he could hear its waves hissing off the shore. It sounded like some great creature breathing gently.

A tingling pain in his wrist made him wince. He rubbed at the skin close to where the metal hook had been inserted into his left arm, where he had lost his own hand as a child. The hook rarely troubled him, except....

Paedur suddenly lifted his left arm, looking at the gleaming half-circle of metal. A twisting, curling design, etched with ancient symbols had been cut into the metal. The runes, as they were called, were usually invisible, but over the years he had noticed that in the presence of magic, they tended to glitter and sparkle slightly.

They were burning brightly now.

With his heart hammering in his chest, Paedur turned. There were two lines of ghostly figures facing him, twelve shapes of mist and shadow. Their edges were indistinct, as if they were being blown away by some invisible wind. The young bard strained to make out details, but only the first figure, the image of a very tall, slender woman was distinct. Paedur got the impression that her features were very delicate, her chin pointed, her eyes sloping slightly upwards. Her hair flowed out behind her in a mass of twisting strands of fog and mist. Her arm, when she lifted it towards the bard, was very thin, her fingers unnaturally long.

'You have no need to fear me ... to fear any of us.' The voice was cold and ghostly in Paedur's head, the words echoing slightly. 'We are powerless now.'

'Who are you?' Paedur asked the fog-shape. He could see that the woman was wearing a style of dress that he had only seen on scraps of ancient pottery.

'We are shadows now,' the woman whispered in his head.

Paedur nodded, 'Who were you?'

The woman half-turned, indicating her companions with a sweep of her overlong arm. 'We were once the Gods of the De Danann people.'

'And you, who are — who were *you*?' Paedur asked, although he had a very good idea.

The ghost's lips twisted into a smile. 'I was once worshipped as the Goddess Danu.'

'My lady!' Paedur said, dropping to both knees and bowing deeply.

'Rise up, young man. I know that the bards still honour me, but few others do. In this modern age, there is little need for gods.'

Paedur came slowly to his feet. The goddess Danu was one of the first of the Old Gods. With the Dagda, she had fashioned the world. 'What happened, my lady?' Paedur asked. 'What happened to you?'

The goddess spread her arms. 'People stopped believing in us. The gods need the human-kind, just as the human-kind need the gods. The more humans who believe in us, the more powerful we become. But when the human-kind find other, newer gods, or things to worship, then our power fades, and we become nothing more than shadows. Ghosts.' She reached out and touched the stone pillars, tracing the spirals with her fingertips. 'These stones contain the first prayers that were ever said to us. Whenever someone touches the stones, traces the designs, as the red-haired boy did, then it is as if a prayer has been uttered to us. It gives us a little power. His prayer allowed us to appear before you.'

'How can we help, lady?' Paedur asked. 'You know that this land is deeply troubled?'

'We know about Balor the Half-Beast. We know that he will destroy this land in his lust for power. He must be stopped.'

'We had already decided that we must try,' Paedur said quietly.

'But perhaps you do not realise the urgency of your mission.' The goddesses voice was stronger now, pounding almost painfully inside the bard's skull. 'Balor has used the Earthlord to destroy those who stand in his way; he caused him to level the city of Gorias only a day ago. But every time the Earthlord calls upon his awesome power, he weakens the very fabric of this island. Already, deep below us, there are great cracks in the heart of the land. The fire mountains that have slept for generations are awake now, the molten stone, which is the blood of this land, had begun to seep to the surface. If the Earthlord continues to tear at this land, then he will set in motion a disaster that will destroy the De Danann Isle, wiping if off the face of the earth!'

Paedur could only stare at the goddess in horror. With the first glimmers of the dawn behind her, she was losing shape and definition. 'Wait, lady,' he called, but it was too late. The fog shape had vanished, only her voice remained echoing inside his head.

'Balor is a fool. His own greed will destroy him. It is not Balor you must stop. It is the Earthlord!'

The people of the city of Falias spoke in whispers of the maze of dungeons that lay deep beneath Balor's palace. Very little was known about them, but there were rumours of a series of hidden tunnels that stretched as far as the coast, so that supplies and troops could be moved in and out of the capital without anyone's knowledge. There were stories of a vast system of streams and canals, of bottomless pits and wells, and there were wild stories of savage blind beasts that roamed the corridors, of hidden traps and hideous non-human guards.

But no-one knew for certain, because no-one had ever escaped from the dungeons. Once prisoners had been led down into the darkness, they were never seen again.

And Colum the Earthlord could understand why.

He was locked in a metal cage in the middle of a fast flowing river that came up to his knees. There were other cages swirling and turning gently in the river, but they were all empty ... except one which had the white skeletal remains of a Fomor still chained to its bars.

Colum shivered. The fast flowing water had numbed the lower half of his body and his teeth were chattering so loudly he thought they were going to break. He knew why Balor had ordered him kept in the middle of the river: he was the Earthlord, he drew his power from the depths of the earth, but he needed to be standing with his bare feet on the ground to be able to draw upon the powerful Elemental magic. He had no control over the element of water; he couldn't work his magic while he was on it, or in it. If he concentrated extraordinarily hard however, he was able to draw up a tiny trickle of energy from the sand and silt beneath his feet, but it was barely enough to keep him warm, and the effort exhausted him.

A metal door clanged in the distance and Colum raised his head tiredly. His eyes were white against his dark skin, and strands of his long black hair were plastered to his face. He was twelve summers old, but his people were smaller than the rest of the De Danann folk, and he was no taller than a fully-grown boy of six or seven summers.

Footsteps echoed in the distance, metal-tipped boots ringing solidly off the stone. Colum knew then that it was either Balor or one of his human troops. The Fomor went bare-footed ... or should that be bare-clawed, he wondered with a slight smile. The smile faded when he wondered what Balor would want him to do next, in exchange for the safety of his mother, and younger brother and sister. Colum knew that if he didn't obey the Emperor's every command, they would be eaten by the serpent-folk.

A figure appeared on the ledge above the river. It was one of Balor's jailers, a giant of a man, with a round, completely hairless head. His eyes were tiny, and bright blood-red. He never spoke. Gripping the winch handle, the jailer turned the massive wheel and the cage lurched up out of the water, tossing Colum from side to side, the metal bars bruising his already tender skin. He clung on tightly while the jailer hauled the cage over the river bank, but the giant allowed the cage to drop the last few feet, the sudden shock knocking the boy to the ground. As he lay there groaning, the door squealed open and the jailer caught the back of his dirty tunic and hauled him out of the cage.

While Colum trooped up the river bank, following the twists and turns of the tunnel system, he attempted to memorise the route. If he ever managed to escape from the cage, he would need to know the way out of the dungeons. They passed cells, some of which were empty, but others held sometimes one, often two or three prisoners. Twice he saw what looked like whole families — mother, father and children — locked up. He wondered what their crime had been.

Balor was waiting for him in the map room, standing with his back to a blazing fire. The Emperor's Fomor blood made him very sensitive to the cold, and when the temperature fell too far, he would become sleepy and slow ... and his temper became very short. He turned more people to stone during the Cold Months than he did at any other time of the year.

There was a Fomor and a female human in the room. Both were standing in the middle of the huge map that covered the floor, the beast holding his spiked tail in one claw so that it wouldn't knock over any of the tiny buildings, or flatten the miniature mountain ranges.

'Aaah, our young Earthlord.' Balor moved away from the fire, rubbing his hands quickly together, the dry skin rasping unpleasantly. The smile on the human half of his face was vicious and ugly.

The woman and the Fomor turned. Colum recognised Cichal by his metal eye patch, but he didn't know the woman. She would have been beautiful, except that her face was hard and expressionless and the colour of old stone. Everything about her was grey: iron-grey hair, cold grey eyes, and her warrior's leather tunic and trousers, and knee high boots were also in grey. She wore a vest of link mail over her tunic and spiked wrist bands on each arm. Two matching heavy-bladed daggers hung on either side of her belt, and Colum could see the hilts of two light swords over either shoulder.

The Emperor put his hand on the Earthlord's shoulder and moved him towards the map. 'You will know Cichal,' he said softly, his voice hissing slightly. 'The woman is Scathach.' He saw Colum's startled look and continued. 'I see the name is familiar to you.'

Colum looked hard at the woman again. All the De Danann Isle knew the name of Scathach the Grey Warrior. The bards told stories about her bravery and skill. Her most famous exploit had taken place ten years previously when she had held back an entire army of savage northern folk by positioning herself on a narrow bridge which they had to pass. She had held the bridge for two days and two nights before help had reached her. She had vanished after that exploit, some said that she had retired, and ran a school for training warriors.

'Cichal and Scathach are going in search of one of your brothers in magic: the Windlord,' Balor continued. 'And they want your help.'

'I have never met the Windlord,' Colum said quickly.

'I know that,' Balor said. 'But you and he are both Lords of the Elemental magic. You became the Earthlord eight summers ago when your father was drowned at sea. The Windlord has only come recently to his power because his uncle trained him in the basics. His skill was improved by his brief stay in Baddalaur. Like you, his father is dead.' Balor's smile was chilling. 'But he does not realise that yet: I turned his parents and sister to stone even before my troops marched through the city gates.' His smiled broadened into a leering grin. 'So all Faolan's previous efforts to save them were for nothing. And soon he will join them,' the Emperor added quickly.

Colum looked up into the half-human face and suddenly realised that the Emperor was afraid of this Windlord and the power he controlled. He bit the inside of his cheek to prevent himself from smiling.

'So now Faolan and his renegades are roaming free on the De Danann Isle. You may have heard rumours of how they defeated me; such stories are untrue. I was betrayed by those I trusted,' he lied. 'Now I want you to find this Windlord for me.' He nodded towards the map. 'Show me where he is.'

Colum shrugged his shoulders. 'My skill is one of working stone and soil, of twisting and turning and shaping the earth to my will. I know nothing about finding people.'

Scathach stepped forward. When she smiled, Colum saw that her teeth had been filed to points, and he remembered that she was supposed to eat her enemies' hearts. He swallowed hard. 'You are the Earthlord,' she said quietly, almost pleasantly. 'You can feel this island, is that not so?'

'This island is a magical place. If I concentrate on any particular part of the island, I can get a sense of that place. If I direct my attention to the Northlands,' Colum pointed to the map at Scathach's feet, 'I will feel cold. If I wished, I could draw up some of the great heat from the interior of the isle and melt the snow ... but that would only disturb the delicate balance of nature in the Northlands.' He paused, and then added. 'But I could not tell you where any individual was in the Northlands.'

'I know that.' Scathach's smile was terrifying. 'But if you can sense this island, if you can feel the magic in this place, then surely you can feel "other" magics disturbing the flow of the natural magic.'

The Earthlord hesitated, then finally nodded. 'It is possible. I've never tried it before.'

Balor's long-nailed fingers tightened on Colum's shoulders. 'Try it now.'

Colum closed his eyes and concentrated on his breathing. He wriggled his toes, feeling the heat from the stones flow up into his body, warming his chest, bringing a flush to his cheeks. He slowly became aware of the stone chamber that surrounded him, of the river flowing far below the palace, of the earth above it, rich dark soil on the stones, of the life moving through the dirt, of the grass above that. It had rained recently and the grass was damp. Trees dug deep into the soil, their roots thick and twisted, mirroring the shape of the branches above. And above the branches the sky.

The Earthlord felt his spirit rise upwards, moving through the soil, up through the tree and out into the air.

Colum felt as if he were flying, rising higher and higher over the island. When he looked down, he didn't see the green and brown of the land, the blue of the sea and the white-tipped mountains. Instead, he saw the colours of life: vibrant reds where the cities and towns clustered, cool blues indicating water, deep purples, like bruises where the soil had been torn and harmed. There was a terrible blackened scar to the west where the Sea of Grass had been burnt. A scattering of purple black stains showed where Balor had forced him to use his magic to hurt the soil and destroy the buildings that clustered on it. Away to the south-west the red colour that marked the city of Gorias was broken by jagged sickly colours, and he knew that disease was running through the city.

But there were other colours in this landscape, whites, greys, ugly yellows, solid blacks: the colours of magic and power. He picked the one nearest the capital, a tiny grey-white spot touched with the white of powerful magic. He allowed his spirit to fall towards it.

Concentrating hard, Colum gradually became aware of his surroundings. He could feel the grittiness of sand beneath his feet, feel the salt breeze on his face. A fire had burnt the soil around it, creating a tiny wound that would soon heal, and the sand insects were already feeding off the remains of fish. The earth was damaged where four or more humans had scooped out beds for themselves in the sand. Trampling feet had crushed grass and sunk into soft damp soil. Concentrating on the damaged soil, Colum sorted through five human sets of tracks — two of them wearing most unusual footwear

— and a beast's paw marks. A pig or a cow perhaps. One of the humans certainly controlled powerful magical forces.

A deep breath shuddered through him and his dark eyes snapped open. For a moment the Emperor's map room swung crazily around him, and he thought he was going to throw up. Breathing deeply, Colum waited until his stomach had stopped fluttering.

'How many are you seeking?' he asked tiredly. 'Is there a beast or an animal amongst them?'

Balor looked triumphantly at Scathach and Cichal. 'One of the Torc Allta walks with them.'

'A boar,' he nodded. 'That makes sense.' He looked up at Scathach. 'To the east of here, I sensed an unusual magic disturbing the atmosphere and soil. When I investigated, I discovered tracks of five humans and a beast. Two of the humans are bootshod, one wears softer moccasins, two are wearing footwear I've never come across before.'

'That's them!' Balor said excitedly. 'That's them; the red-haired humans from the time to come would be wearing unusual shoes.'

'Where are they?' Cichal hissed.

'On the Avenue of Standing Stones.'

'Destroy it,' Balor grunted. 'Destroy it now!'

Sitting by the side of a rock pool, washing her face in cold salt water, Ally remembered what she disliked about the De Danann Isle.

Six months previously, when Ally and Ken had returned from the De Danann Isle, they had decided not to tell anyone about their adventures: who would have believed them anyway? They had talked about it constantly in the beginning, but as time went by, they found other things to occupy their thoughts: return to school, new subjects and new teachers, and then the Christmas exams and holidays. They hadn't spoken about their adventures in weeks.

And now Ally discovered that her memory had played a trick on her. Whenever she thought of the island, she had only remembered the excitement, the extraordinary magic, the fabulous beasts and creatures. She had forgotten that there were no bathrooms, no hot water, no electric fires, no instant food. She hadn't remembered the flies, the countless biting, stinging insects, the smells of her unwashed companions, the stink of her own clothing.

She hadn't remembered that she had spent much of the time afraid, frightened of everyone and everything.

When the Fomor had appeared at their window and chased them through the house, her only thought had been to escape the beast. She knew the pendants of frozen air the Windlord had given them would pull them through time to the De Danann Isle. There the bard would know what to do; Ragallach would protect them with his great strength, Megan's fighting skills would keep them safe, and then Faolan would be able to use his magic to send them back.

Now that she was back however, she was beginning to think that she had made a terrible mistake. After all, her friends were only three humans and a were-beast against the might of the Emperor's reptilian army.

Ragallach came and squatted down beside her. With the coming of dawn, he had assumed his were-shape, a mixture of man and beast. Even though he crouched down, Ally had to look up to his enormous pig-like face. 'I know you humans find it difficult to read our expressions,' he grunted, his flat moist nose wrinkling. 'And we beasts find it hard to make out what you human-kind are thinking. But I do know that you are troubled.'

Ally reached out and rubbed Ragallach's hairy arm. The orange bristles were surprisingly soft. 'I'm frightened,' she admitted.

'There is no shame in being frightened,' the Torc Allta said. 'The shame comes when one is frightened over nothing.' He bared his tusks in a terrifying grimace, which Ally had come to recognise as a grin. 'You have good cause to fear.'

'I was thinking of asking Faolan to send us back to our own time,' she said softly, glancing back down the beach, to where the others were scattering the remains of the previous night's fire and burying the fishbones, leaving no trace that anyone had ever been there.

Ragallach nodded. 'You could do that. But remember, Balor sent a Fomor to slay you once — he will do so again.'

'Do you think so?'

'There are many stories told about the Emperor; you should ask the bard to tell you some of them. But there are no gentle stories to his name, no mention of an act of kindness, or compassion. He is the son of a human mother and a Fomor father. His mother was a witch, cruel and evil, his father a fearsome and savage warrior without pity or mercy. Balor takes after both his parents. He will not rest until he has destroyed us all, and has our heads as proof. You will be no safer if you return to your own time. In fact, you will probably be in even greater danger: here we can protect you, but in your time, you will have nothing.'

Ally swallowed hard. 'Maybe we should stay.'

'We will look after you...' Ragallach began, and then stopped. He raised his huge head, tilted it to one side, listening.

'What is it?' Ally asked, her voice falling to a whisper.

The Torc Allta shook his head. 'Something in the distance,' he muttered, 'like thunder ... except that it is not thunder.'

The girl scrambled to her feet. She climbed over the stones, and pulled herself to the top of the tallest sand dune, shading her eyes, staring back across the land. 'I can't see anything,' she said, 'except for some clouds in the distance.'

'Where are the clouds?' Ragallach asked.

'I can see the line of the ancient road in the distance,' Ally said. 'The cloud seems to be concentrated on the road.' She looked back at the Torc Allta. 'Is something wrong?'

He shook his huge head. 'I don't know,' he said slowly.

'The cloud is coming nearer,' Ally said suddenly. She slid down the sand dune. 'There's something on the road. Something coming,' she added breathlessly.

Ragallach turned and raced back toward their companions, Ally following more slowly, picking her way across the slippery stones. She could hear a sound now, a rumbling, grumbling grating, grinding noise, like two massive stones being rubbed together. She could hear Ragallach shouting, but with the sea wind whipping away his words and the thunderous rumbling behind her, she was sure none of the others would be able to hear him. Over the sand dunes she could see that the cloud was almost upon them. The noise was incredible; the air itself was vibrating with sound. The ground was trembling, stones tumbling and falling, sand dunes crumbling, the waves churning into a frenzy. She fell to the ground, clutching at the beach, digging her fingers deep into the soft soil as she felt the earth shift and move beneath her. Panic-stricken, she turned around, desperately looking for something solid to hold onto. She saw the ancient road rise up, like a shaken piece of cloth, the smooth stones thrown high into the air. They fell back onto the beach and shattered into razor sharp fragments which whined through the air. The road split in two, a deep v-shaped pit opening beneath it, as if a knife had been plunged into the earth and dragged along its length. The water boiled in white fury as the destruction ripped out beneath the waves.

Ally staggered to her feet. She could barely stand, but she wasn't sure if the ground was still trembling or if it was her own shaking legs. She opened her mouth and screamed — but her own voice sounded faint and distant, and then she realised that she couldn't hear the sound of the sea. The incredible noise had deafened her.

She found Ragallach first, half buried in sand and dirt. His eyes were closed and for a terrifying moment, she thought he was dead. But when she touched him, his pink eyes snapped open and his snout flared. He pushed himself to his feet in a flurry of grit and sand, and the girl could see his mouth moving as he spoke. Ally touched her ears and screamed, 'I can't hear you. I'm deaf.'

The beast leaned forward and bellowed in Ally's ear. 'It will wear off soon.'

They found Megan next. She was sitting with her back to one of the ancient standing stones, which was now split right down the middle. There was a cut on her forehead and blood streamed from her nose. Ally dabbed at the cut on the girl's forehead with her handkerchief; she had been hit with a flying rock, and it was already rising to a purple bump.

Paedur was helping Faolan to his feet as Ragallach and the two girls picked their way through the debris. The bard was completely coated in white dust, while Faolan was splashed with thick, foul-smelling black muck. Neither seemed hurt.

'Earthmagic,' Paedur said bitterly, as the others joined them. 'This Earthlord had destroyed one of the oldest sites in the De Danann Isle, just to kill us.'

'Where's Ken,' Ally asked, looking around. There was a sudden sour feeling in the pit of her stomach.

'I thought he was with you,' Paedur said, startled.

Ally shook her head. 'He was with you.'

'He had been going to find you when the earthquake struck,' Paedur said.

Ragallach's paw fell onto Ally's shoulder and squeezed comfortingly. 'We'll find him.'

Megan wrapped her arms around Ally, holding her while she trembled with a mixture of shock and dread. She was too frightened to talk.

Faolan and Paedur took up positions on either side of Ragallach, their faces grave and worried. The Torc Allta lifted his head high, his snout wrinkling as he tested the air for scents. 'Nothing,' he grunted. The trio moved quickly through the jumble that had once been the road, calling Ken's name, while Ragallach tested the air for the boy's odour.

'Here!' Paedur suddenly shouted.

Ally broke free of Megan's arms and raced down the beach to where Faolan and Paedur were helping Ragallach pull away a pile of stones. Faolan caught Ally as she ran up and held her back. 'It's

Ken,' he said, his voice quivering slightly. 'He's been hurt, but he's alive.'

'I want to see him,' Ally struggled away from the Windlord and fell to her knees, looking into the deep hole where Ken lay. He was still and unmoving, his face deathly pale. There was blood on his lips. Ragallach was squatting in the hole, pulling off small rocks and stones, as he tried to dig him out.

Paedur knelt beside her and put his arm around her shoulder. 'The force of the earthquake opened up this long tear in the earth. When Ken fell into it, paving slabs from the road and boulders fell in on top of him.' He pointed with his hook. 'He was saved from certain death because one of the tall standing stones lodged sideways in the hole; that stopped everything from crashing in on top of him.'

Ally gripped Paedur's hand tightly. 'We've got to get him out.'

'We will,' the bard promised.

The Torc Allta climbed up from the hole, shaking his head. 'Every time I move something, the whole lot threatens to cave in and crush him. I daren't risk touching anything else.'

'Give me a moment to think...' Paedur began.

Megan tapped his shoulder and pointed to the waves, which were already beginning to creep up the beach. 'We don't have much time. The tide is coming in. And it will fill the hole,' she said quietly, hoping Ally couldn't hear her.

Ally heard every word.

The sky above Falias came alive with the sound of snapping, clapping wings as ten nathair took to the air. The enormous flying serpents swooped low over the city, their wingtips almost brushing the tops of the tallest houses, before their riders adjusted the hoods which covered the creatures' eyes, allowing in a little light. The nathair immediately swung around towards the light, heading towards the east ... towards the Avenue of Standing Stones.

Cichal rode the first of the black nathair, sitting awkwardly in the high wooden saddle. He preferred riding his own mount, but these were the Emperor's personal nathair, bred for speed rather than strength. Their bat-like wings had been tipped with metal, as had their claws and a spiked ball had been fitted to the tip of their tails. He glanced back over his shoulder; Scathach followed on the second nathair, a scarf wrapped around her mouth and nose, and the Fomor suddenly remembered that the humans found the smell of nathair revolting. Behind her came eight more nathair, all bearing Fomor, the pick of his Troop. He had also included his hatchling Goll, amongst them. It was only fitting that he should be one of those who captured these renegades, including the red-haired demons.

Scathach urged her mount nearer Cichal's. The two serpents, sensing one another's presence, lashed out with their tails. Caught off balance, the Grey Warrior almost tumbled to the ground.

'Stay back,' Cichal called. 'Even at the best of times, these creatures are ill tempered, and these are the Emperor's own nathair: they hate everyone.'

Scathach nodded. 'How close are we now?'

The Fomor glanced into the sky. 'We'll be there before noon.'

Scathach laughed humourlessly. 'Perhaps all we'll have to do will be to pick up the bodies.'

Cichal said nothing. He had fought these renegades before. And lost. He had learned to respect them.

'Windmagic,' Faolan said simply. 'We will have to call upon my windlore.'

'But that will alert the Emperor to our presence,' Megan protested.

'The Emperor already knows we're here,' Paedur remarked. 'That's why he had the Earthlord destroy the ancient road.' He turned to look up into the sky. 'I wouldn't be at all surprised if he had Fomor on nathair on their way here already.'

'Hurry,' Ally insisted tearfully. Ken hadn't moved, hadn't responded when she shouted his name. And the hissing white foam was creeping slowly up the beach.

Paedur nodded to Faolan. 'Do it.'

'Stand back,' Faolan said. He waited until the others had moved back to the sand dunes before he stepped up to the pile of tumbled stone where Ken lay trapped. Holding his hands loosely by his side, he closed his eyes and bent his head. Breathing evenly and deeply, he concentrated on calling up the ancient magic that his family had guarded for generations.

Faolan's long golden hair began to flutter in a breeze which none of the others felt. Grains of sand twisted and turned around his feet, and his clothing began to flap in the magical breeze.

The Windlord raised his hands.

A stiff breeze immediately began to blow in off the sea, churning it to a white froth. Sand hissed and whispered along the beach as the wind rose.

'I can smell herbs and spices,' Megan whispered.

'Faolan calls the wind from other parts of this world,' Paedur murmured.

'Look!' Ragallach grunted.

The wind was now howling around Faolan. He stretched his arms out from his body, palm downwards ... and the wind flowed into his hands. Beneath his open palms the sand was churned to a frenzy as two smooth circles were carved away, golden grains spinning out on all sides.

Faolan took a step closer to the pit.

The Windlord directed his power onto the tumbled stones. The lighter sand and dirt was blown away instantly, the heavier blocks and stones trembled and shuddered before they too finally shifted and moved, the elemental power of the wind simply tossing them away.

The first trickle of the incoming tide dribbled into the pit.

Faolan redoubled his efforts, calling upon the power of the storm, the typhoon, the hurricane and the tempest. The ghost wind no longer smelt sweet, now it was cold and bitter, sharp with ice and snow. Instead of lifting the stones and tossing them away, it pulverised the smaller ones to dust, cracking the bigger rocks in two, then breaking them again and again, before grinding them to powder. Within moments, Faolan had cleared most of the rubble that covered Ken; only two of the taller pillars remained. The young Windlord lowered his hands and the wind died. Stepping back from the pit, Faolan slumped to the ground, exhausted.

'I can do no more,' he whispered as the others ran up. 'I'm afraid if I break the last two stones, they will fall onto Ken and crush him.'

Paedur knelt by the edge of the pit and squeezed Faolan's shoulder. 'You've done enough.' He looked up at the Torc Allta, his eyebrows raised in a silent question.

Ragallach nodded. The were-beast climbed down into the pit and took hold of the first of the ancient pillars. It was almost as tall as the beast, and easily as thick. It had snapped off close to the ground and the earthquake had shaken off much of the dust and dirt that had coated it, allowing the twisting, curling, spiral writing to show clearly. The Torc Allta heaved, his muscles straining, veins appearing on the back of his arms and across his shoulders. With an enormous effort he lifted the enormous stone above his head and heaved it onto the beach. The second stone covering Ken was shorter, but thicker.

'You lift it,' Paedur said, climbing down into the pit alongside Ragallach. 'And I'll pull Ken out.'

The Torc Allta caught one end of the stone, planted his hooves firmly and heaved. The stone came up out of the sand and mud with a liquid gurgling. Paedur caught Ken's shoulders and dragged him out, passing him back up to Ally and Megan who hauled him onto the beach.

Ally knelt on the sand with her brother's head on her lap. He was only barely breathing, and there was a bump the size of an egg just above his ear. She wasn't aware of the tears streaming down her face as she brushed his matted hair. They squabbled and fought constantly, and at times she hated him, but it was only now, looking at him so small and frail, that she realised just how much he meant to her.

Paedur tilted Ally's chin up and looked into her tear-filled eyes. 'We'll get help. He's strong. He'll be all right.' He spoke so confidently that Ally found herself believing him. She didn't see the doubt in Paedur's dark eyes.

'There!' Cichal pointed downwards, and Scathach leaned over the nathair's saddle to look down onto the earth below. Where the ancient Avenue of Standing Stones had run was now nothing more than a long line of devastation. She could see clearly where the road had been split right down the middle. For the first time the Grey Warrior realised just how powerful Colum was. She shuddered. Like most warriors, she detested magic: it could not be fought with a blade or spear, it could kill at a distance. It was a coward's weapon. She closed her right hand into a fist, sticking out her little and index fingers: the Sign of Horns was supposed to keep away evil magic.

Cichal brought the nathair lower, until the serpent's wings were raising dust from the ruins below. In the distance, he could see the long blue line of the sea. If everything went according to plan he would have the renegades in moments.

Ragallach climbed up out of the pit in a flurry of sand. 'Nathair,' he grunted, snout wrinkling. 'Nathair coming.' He pointed back along the shattered road.

The ten nathair came in low over the dunes even as he was speaking, wings spread wide, jaws gaping. Their riders carried long spears and one, a human woman, was notching a bow. Paedur's sharp eyesight recognised Cichal by his metal eyepatch. The Fomor Officer opened his mouth and screamed in triumph.

Faolan surged to his feet and raised his hands....

An enormous column of sand erupted beneath the leading nathair. It exploded against its scaly chest, pushing it back up into the air, disturbing the rhythm of its wings. It crashed back into the second nathair, which immediately bit at it with its razor-sharp teeth. Both serpents tumbled to the ground in a flurry of leathery wings.

Another column of solid sand and grit speared up into the midst of the flying serpents, toppling riders and nathair to the ground. The temperamental serpents immediately began fighting amongst themselves, lashing out with wings and tails, snapping with teeth.

More and more of the sand columns exploded amongst the confused creatures, driving them to a frenzy.

Faolan's golden hair was wild about his face. Without turning around, he called, 'Catch one of the nathair. I'll keep them busy.' He moved his hand in a broad sweeping gesture, calling down the wind, blinding the beasts with stinging sand, hurling rocks and stones at them. Another scattering of sand explosions rippled along the beach as Faolan's power sucked up the sand, then sent it spinning around the terrified creatures.

Ragallach and Paedur raced down the beach to where one of the nathair was crouched, shivering but unmoving. As they got closer, they realised that its hood had fallen over its eyes, blinding it. Unable to see, the nathair simply sat still, occasionally hissing at the sand which slid beneath its scales irritating it.

Paedur vaulted into the high wooden saddle and worked the reins, raising the left side of the hood, allowing a little light in. The serpent immediately turned in that direction, its muscular body rippling as it pushed forward.

Scathach suddenly ran out of the dust storm, a bow in her hand. She spotted the bard and raised the bow, pulling the cord back to her cheek.

And then a monster rose up before her, massive jaws gaping, dripping saliva. It roared at her, snatching the bow from her hands, crushing it to splinters, pushing her back into the twisting sand storm. The wind caught her, spun her around, sucking her back into the confusion as she struggled to free her sword.

Ragallach dropped the remains of the bow and hurried off after the nathair, which the bard was guiding back to the rest of the group.

It was only when the sand storm had died and the Fomor had finally got their crazed beasts under control, that Cichal realised that one of the nathair — his own nathair! — was missing. And so were the renegades. Cichal hissed savagely. They had won again ... but the Fomor were patient, he would wait. They would make a mistake, and he would have them then.

Paedur guided the black nathair back towards the capital. He kept the creature close to the ground, just above the tree tops. The nathair was carrying the weight of five humans and a Torc Allta and he knew it would tire quickly. He wanted to be able to bring it in to land at the first signs of tiredness.

The bard glanced back over his shoulder. Ken was still unconscious and both he and Faolan, who had collapsed from exhaustion, were tied to the nathair just behind its wings. Megan and Ally lay flat along the creature's back behind its wings where they could hold onto Ken and Faolan. Ragallach sat behind the bard, his three-toed hooves clutching the wooden frame of the saddle. Resting his head against the back of the high backed seat, the Torc Allta murmured in Paedur's ear.

'I fear for the boy.'

'So do I.'

'Do you know any physicians in Falias?'

Paedur shook his head. 'The only healer I know of is Diancecht.'

Ragallach bared his tusks in a quick grin. 'I thought Diancecht was the Emperor's private physician.'

'He is.'

The Torc Allta's bristles tickled Paedur's ear as the beast murmured. 'Tell me how we are going to get the Emperor's personal healer to look after Ken?'

Paedur shrugged. He turned his head to look into Ragallach's pink eyes. 'We'll ask him, very politely.'

'And if he refuses?' the Torc Allta wondered.

'We'll ask him again ... only not so politely.'

Diancecht the Healer claimed that he could trace his family's history back to the time when the first of the De Danann race had walked this world. He was a small, stout man, completely bald, though he still had a full white beard which fell almost to his waist, and his eyebrows too were snow white, beneath which his eyes were a startling vivid blue. His father had been a healer and his father before him, in an unbroken tradition going back generations. Diancecht was determined that his own son, Miach, would also become a healer.

But, whereas Diancecht's father had treated everyone, young and old, wealthy and poor, not caring whether they could pay or not, Diancecht had made his fortune attending to the rich. He was the personal physician to most of Falias' aristocracy, including the Emperor himself. He was the only physician capable of easing the great pains that sometimes twisted Balor's body, the terrible headaches that often blinded him, and the aches that stiffened his legs so that he was incapable of walking. The healer had tried to explain to the Emperor that the pains were caused by Balor's mixed Fomor and human blood, but the Emperor wasn't interested; he just wanted the pain taken away. Balor had made Diancecht wealthy, loading him with gifts in return for his healing, but instead of being satisfied with his great wealth, Diancecht had become even greedier. And his greed and position of power had made him a person to be feared.

Diancecht sat in the courtyard of his palace in Falias every day from dawn until noon, seeing patients. Often those who came to him were not actually ill, but simply wanted to ask his advice about the Emperor, or to request that he should find their sons or daughters a position at court, or to suggest that the Imperial palace might buy meat or fruit or wines from them. If they were willing to pay his fat fee, then Diancecht could arrange all sorts of matters.

In the afternoons, Diancecht bathed in a huge hot pool in a sunny courtyard at the back of his palace. The warm water seeped up from an enormous hot pool that bubbled deep beneath the city, and the water never froze, even in the depths of the Cold Months.

Diancecht stepped into the warm, slightly steaming water. He always added special herbs and spices before he bathed. The herbs refreshed his skin and helped keep him young, and the spices disguised the slightly bitter, rotten-egg odour of the water.

Taking a deep breath, squeezing his eyes shut, the physician ducked his head beneath the water, rubbing his bald skull vigorously. He believed that if he massaged his head with the hot water, his hair would begin to grow again. If it didn't, he had a special paste of cow dung, fresh eggs and mashed fruit; it smelled revolting, but he thought it might work. Lifting his head from the water, he patted at his stinging eyes with a towel, then lay back in the water, floating with the sun in his eyes, and allowed himself to doze off to sleep. He was calculating how much he had made today.

Paedur brought the nathair to a stop in a field outside of Falias, at the edge of the ancient woods. While Ragallach helped everyone off, Paedur adjusted the flying serpent's hood, cutting through the thick stitching with the edge of his hook. When he jumped to the ground, he jerked the hood a little allowing light to seep in from the top. The nathair immediately took off into the sky, its powerful wings lifting it higher and higher. The vibrations of its flight shook loose the rest of the stitching on its hood, and the entire covering fell away. Completely confused, the nathair flew around in a circle, rising higher and higher into the sky, until it was nothing more than a black dot.

Ragallach shaded his small eyes with his hoof. 'What will happen to it?'

'It will get tired eventually,' Paedur said, 'and when the light fades, it will return to its nest in Falias. That gives us some time to get inside the city before the nathair returns.'

'Have you a plan?' Megan asked, joining them.

Paedur pointed towards a tumbled cottage that was almost lost beneath the trees. It looked derelict, except for the thin thread of grey smoke that rose out of its crooked chimney. There was an abandoned wagon half-filled with mouldering hay alongside the cottage. 'I want you and Faolan to go over there and buy some clothes for Ken and Ally, and then buy that wagon and hay.'

Megan shrugged. 'It would be easier to steal it.'

Paedur nodded. 'It would. But what would happen if the theft was reported? The Watch would be on the look out for the wagon. No, offer to buy it. I'm sure they'll sell.'

'And if they don't?' Megan insisted.

'Offer them more money!' Paedur snapped, turning away. He went and knelt by Ken's side, pressing a hand to the boy's chest, his delicate fingers feeling the fluttering of his heart in his chest. His breathing was still shallow and fast and the bump on his head was turning a rich purple-red. When Paedur pushed back Ken's eyelid, only the white was showing.

'He's going to die, isn't he?' Ally whispered. She had been crying and her red eyes stood out vividly against the paleness of her face.

Ragallach squatted down behind Ally and put his arm on her shoulder. 'We're taking him to a healer now.'

'Is he good this healer?'

'The best,' Ragallach smiled. 'He is the Emperor's private physician.'

'Is there no magic you could use?' Ally asked desperately.

Paedur shook his head. 'Using magic on another human is dangerous. The body can be tricked into thinking it is well, but that doesn't send the disease or the injury away. I'm sure I could bring Ken awake, but who knows what damage I might be doing to him? No, let him sleep. His body is protecting itself while he sleeps. The healer will do the rest.'

'But what if this healer refuses to help?' Ally asked, echoing the question the Torc Allta had asked earlier.

'He won't,' Paedur and Ragallach said together.

Faolan and Megan returned with the cart which they had bought — very cheaply — from the old woman who lived in the cottage. If she wondered what the young couple wanted with a cart full of mouldy hay, she didn't ask.

Ragallach lifted Ken gently into the back of the cart and then, with Ally riding alongside her brother, the Torc Allta pulled it until they were in sight of Falias' walls. By then the sun was sinking, and he could feel the were-change beginning to creep in upon him. 'Your brother will be well again,' he managed to say before his body twisted and changed into that of a pig.

'We shall have to be very careful now,' Paedur said. He lifted the pig into the back of the cart, where it snuggled in alongside Ken.

'We should try to arrive at the city gates just before they close. The guards are usually so eager to go off duty that they rarely check the latecomers. Faolan, keep your head low, and try to speak like an old man. Megan, Ally, huddle together on the cart and keep your heads low. If you are asked any questions, whisper your answers like tired old women.'

'That will never fool them,' Megan said quickly.

'Every day they see many carts like this, pulled by old men with old women sitting on the back. When they look at you that's what they'll expect to see ... so that's what they *will* see.'

Megan nodded, unconvinced. She pulled the smelly ruin of a dress she had bought at the cottage over Ally's head, and tucked her bright red hair beneath a floppy brimmed hat. Finally, she streaked the girl's face and hands with mud. Standing back, she looked at Ally and grimaced. 'You don't look like an old woman,' she said, 'you look like a young woman with a dirty face.'

Ally sniffed at the sleeve of the dress. 'It's disgusting; I think I'm going to throw up.'

Paedur walked over to Faolan, who was staring at Falias' high walls. In the last rays of the sinking sun, the gold covered roofs blazed with warm orange light. 'Do you think you can pull the cart to the gate?' Paedur asked. 'I'll have to hide in the cart with Ken and Ragallach, because I'm too well known, so you'll be pulling the weight of the cart and the five of us.'

The young Windlord looked at the distance to the nearest gate and smiled doubtfully. 'You know I'll try. But the effort of calling the wind twice today has exhausted me. All I want to do is sleep.'

Paedur reached out and touched Faolan with his hook. The half circle of metal grew warm, and the Windlord immediately felt strength flow into him. 'Get us through the gate,' Paedur said, 'and you can spend the night in a soft bed.' Faolan looked doubtful, but the bard nodded. 'I swear it.'

As night fell over Falias, just before the city gates closed for the night, a battered wooden cart piled with hay, pulled by a bent old man, with two equally old woman in the cart, made its way into the city. The guards passed the cart through the gates quickly, disgusted by the smell of manure and rotten straw it carried with it.

As the cart turned into the nearest alleyway, the massive iron and stone gates clanged shut for the night, sealing the city.

Diancecht slept in scented sheets of the softest wool, on a pillow stuffed with herbs which were supposed to bring pleasant dreams. If he woke during the night there was a pitcher of chilled water and some fresh fruit by his bedside, and a bell to call the servants who slept at the other end of the house.

Usually the healer slept well, but tonight he couldn't settle. He tossed and turned, unable to make himself comfortable: the sheets were scratchy, the pillow lumpy — even the herbs smelt slightly sour. Diancecht sat up in bed and lifted the pillow, pressing his face into its softness, inhaling the slightly bitter odours of mint and thyme. He wondered if there was another odour in the room...?

When Diancecht lowered the pillow, a cold metal blade was pressed to his cheek. 'Don't say a word,' an invisible voice commanded. Someone moved in the darkness behind him, and Diancecht realised there was more than one person in the room with him. And he realised where the unpleasant odour was coming from now: these thieves stank.

A flint struck metal and a spark winked in the darkness. Light flared, and Diancecht suddenly saw the person who was sitting on the edge of his bed, holding a knife before him ... only it wasn't a knife, it was a hook that took the place of his left hand. The healer's bright blue eyes opened wide in understanding....

'I see you've recognised me,' Paedur said, very quietly. 'I am Paedur the bard, and these are my companions, Faolan, Megan and the red-haired girl is Ally. The boy on the floor is her brother Ken, who was injured when the Emperor used the Earthlord to attack us.' In the flickering lamplight, Paedur's smile was icy. 'We want you to heal Ken.'

'Impossible,' Diancecht blustered. 'I will do no such thing. You are renegades with a price on your heads.'

Megan came and knelt by Diancecht's bed. With the lamplight

flickering across her dirty face, she looked savage and wild. Without saying a word she lifted a long flat-bladed knife with a white bone handle and looked at Paedur, eyebrows raised in a silent question.

The bard shook his head slightly. 'This is Megan,' he said to Diancecht. 'She comes from a village in the Ice Fields of Thusal. Do you know,' he added, 'that some of the villagers are cannibals?'

Diancecht looked at Megan and swallowed hard. 'Is she a cannibal?' he whispered.

'We haven't eaten properly in days,' Paedur smiled. 'I'm sure she's hungry.'

'I'm hungry,' Megan said hoarsely, in a thick accent. She had to bite the inside of her cheek to stop herself from laughing at Diancecht's horrified expression.

Paedur glanced across the room to where Ally sat, cradling Ken's head in her lap. 'I suggest you should heal our friend while I take Megan down to the kitchens to get something to eat.'

The healer nodded quickly, his bald head bobbing.

'No tricks,' Paedur warned.

Diancecht shook his head, eyes flickering from the bard to the warrior maid. He started when Faolan appeared behind the bard. The boy stretched out his hand, moving his fingers slightly, and the healer felt an icy breeze blow across his sweating face.

'If you try anything, Faolan will use his windmagic to carry you to the ends of the earth,' the bard added.

'Or into the heart of a fire-mountain,' Faolan whispered.

Diancecht swallowed hard. 'No tricks,' he promised. Throwing back the sheets, he swung his legs out of bed. 'What happened?' he asked, kneeling on the floor beside Ken, his long delicate fingers probing the bump on the side of his head.

'We believe he was struck by a rock,' Paedur said. 'He was buried under a pile of stones.'

Diancecht stood. 'Can you carry him down to my healing chamber?'

The bard nodded. Crouching behind Ken, he carefully lifted his shoulders, while Faolan carried his legs. Megan picked up the small lamp and helped Ally to her feet.

'Follow me,' Diancecht said.

Megan touched the healer's arm, her hand closing over his plump flesh. 'Remember, no tricks,' she whispered, 'or I'll be forced to eat those nice fingers of yours.'

Diancecht immediately closed his hands into tight fists. 'No tricks,' he promised again.

Diancecht's healing chamber was in the very heart of the house. An enormous circular room had been built around a long narrow pool. Everything was white; white flagstone floor, white ceiling, polished white walls. The room was filled with candles and mirrors, and Paedur guessed that when the sun shone through the high arched windows, the room would blaze with light.

'Put him here,' Diancecht commanded, indicating a long table beside the bath. 'Light the candles,' he added.

Paedur caught Ally's hand and drew her toward the first bank of candles. He lit one from the lamp which Megan carried and handed it to Ally. Without a word, she began to light the candles. The bard watched her for a moment and then turned back to Megan. 'There must be servants in this house. Use your sleeping honey to make sure they don't wake too soon.'

The warrior maid nodded. She reached into her belt and took out a handful of her green-tipped darts.

'Oh, and Megan,' Paedur smiled. 'Perhaps it would be better if you cleaned yourself up before you went after them.'

Megan held up the front of her jerkin and smelled it. 'Maybe if my sleeping darts don't knock them out, then the smell will. I'll use the pool in the courtyard.'

'And get yourself some food too,' the bard added. 'I'll send Faolan and Ally after you when they've finished with the candles.'

'What about you?' Megan asked.

'I'll keep an eye on our nervous healer. I'll get something when everyone comes back. Where's Ragallach?' he asked.

'When I last saw him, he was swimming in the pool in the courtyard.'

Paedur nodded. 'It will be dawn soon. When he's back into his were-shape he can look after Diancecht while the rest of us get some sleep. Now go. Send everyone to sleep. We don't want any surprises.'

Megan nodded, and slipped out into the night.

Paedur walked over to Diancecht who had stripped off Ken's filthy cloak and was now looking at the clothes the boy was wearing.

'I've never seen garments like these,' he said, touching the denim jeans. 'And the boy's hair — like the girl's — is red. I've never known a human to have red hair. Are they related to the Small Folk?'

Paedur shook his head. 'No, they are human-kind, but from a time many thousands of seasons in the future.'

'Are they powerful magicians then?' Diancecht asked, beginning to undo the buttons on Ken shirt.

'They have no magic,' the bard said quietly.

'But why does Balor fear them?'

Paedur shrugged. 'Why does he fear any of us?' he asked.

Diancecht looked at Paedur in surprise. 'Surely you know? He fears you because you are free and because you do not fear him. He rules through fear; he cannot rule those who are not frightened of him.' He dipped a cloth into the warm water in the pool and began to wash the dirt from Ken's body.

'But we all fear Balor,' Paedur said surprised.

Diancecht nodded. 'But even though you fear him, you are still fighting him. You have learned to conquer your fear of the man.'

'I fear what he is doing to this island,' Paedur murmured. The candle-light, now reflected and magnified by the mirrors, made his face look yellow and old. 'This was once a united place, an island where men and beasts lived peacefully together. Now, Balor has driven a wedge between the human-kind and the Fomor. He wants all the magic in the world so that he can rule with it. He has changed ancient magic, pure magic into something evil. Yesterday, he used the Earthlord's power to destroy the Avenue of Standing Stones.'

Diancecht frowned. 'But that place is sacred to the old gods.'

'Do you still worship the old gods?' Paedur asked surprised.

'I am a healer. I worship the Dagda,' Diancecht said proudly.

'The Avenue of Standing Stones has stood for a hundred generations. Balor had it destroyed simply to slay us.'

Diancecht frowned. 'That is not right.' He bent over Ken, turning his head slightly, the fingers of his left hand busy around the boy's head, while his right hand rested lightly on his chest, feeling his fluttering heartbeat.

'Why should you care?' Paedur asked, 'you are the Emperor's man.'

'I was not always the Emperor's man,' Diancecht said very

quietly. He bent and lifted Ken with surprising ease and lowered him into the narrow pool.

Ally ran over to the side of the pool. 'What are you doing?' she demanded.

'These waters contain healing herbs and salts,' Diancecht said. 'When they have been absorbed into your brother's skin, they will help the healing process.'

'Is he going to be all right?'

Diancecht smiled, and then said proudly. 'I am the finest healer on the De Danann Isle, of course he will be all right!'

Paedur looked at Faolan. 'Why don't you and Ally get something to eat. You could clean yourselves up also.'

'I want to stay,' Ally said quickly.

'There's no point,' Paedur said. 'Healing takes time. And I need you well and rested for the morrow.'

Faolan put his arm around Ally's shoulder and led her from the room.

Kneeling by the side of the pool, Diancecht applied a green paste to the bump on the side of Ken's head. Without looking up, he said, 'What do you hope to achieve? You are so few and the Emperor is powerful. You cannot hope to defeat him.'

The young bard sat on the edge of the pool and trailed his hand in the warm water. 'We defeated him once before,' he reminded the healer.

'Do you know that Cichal and Scathach the Grey Warrior and eight highly trained Fomor have been given the task of tracking you down?'

'We met them,' Paedur said shortly. 'We had just pulled Ken out from the ruin of the Avenue of Standing Stones when we were attacked by ten nathair. Cichal and the woman were amongst them.'

'And you defeated them?' Diancecht asked, astonished.

'We flew here on one of their nathair,' the bard grinned.

The healer started to laugh, a low chuckle that gradually grew louder, until it echoed and re-echoed around the chamber. He finally stopped, breathless and with tears streaming down his face.

'What's so funny?' Paedur asked.

'I was just imagining Balor's face when Cichal made his report.' He started laughing again, and this time the bard joined in.

Balor stood by the window of the high tower that speared into the sky over his palace and watched nine black nathair flying in from the east. One was carrying two riders.

The Emperor turned away from the window, feeling rage building up inside him. He had sent Cichal with eight Fomor and the deadly Scathach after the renegades ... and they had been defeated. Throwing back his head, Balor screamed aloud his rage, the sound bouncing back off the bare stone walls, until it sounded like the howling of a pack of savage animals.

And all those who heard the roar suddenly discovered that they had business far away from the palace. No-one wanted to face the Emperor when he was in such ill-humour; no-one wanted to join the hundreds of frozen statues that lined his halls.

Cichal prepared himself to die.

Before he made his report to the Emperor, he had gone to his chamber and gathered up his few belongings — his spare eye-patch, the fleecy woollen cloak his mother had sent him, the stone paintings of his hatchlings and his mate. He had looked at the image of Moriath, his mate, for a long time. The artist had caught her picture perfectly, the shimmering green of her scales, the brightness of her yellow eyes, the pinkness of her tongue, her perfect needle-pointed teeth. She was the most beautiful of the Fomor, and his only regret now was that he had not spent more time with her and his hatchlings. He wrapped everything in a blanket and then, taking a flat square of soft metal, he scratched a quick note with his sharp nails to Goll, his eldest hatchling, instructing him to return everything to the Fomor Isles.

Taking a last look around the chamber, Cichal stepped out of the room and pulled the heavy door shut behind him. He didn't bother locking it: he didn't expect to be coming back. Cichal stood in the centre of the corridor and straightened his leather jerkin, hitching his stone sword higher on his shoulder. His tail was twitching nervously, but he forced it to remain still. He paused for a moment, rubbing a scrap of cloth across his metallic eye patch until it gleamed. When he was finally satisfied with his appearance, he set off to meet the Emperor.

He wondered what it would be like to be turned to stone.

Balor prowled around his chamber like a caged beast. His shoulders were hunched, his hands locked into claws, his mouth open in a savage grimace, exposing his triangular, razor sharp teeth.

Scathach stood calmly before the blazing fire, warming herself while she drank a cup of thick mead. She smacked her lips, licking the last of the thick honey drink from the bottom of the cup. 'There was nothing anyone could have done,' she said reasonably. 'When we arrived the place had been devastated by an earthquake, but before we could land we were attacked by the Windlord's magic.' She shrugged. 'We could not fight that. He sent sand and stones up amongst the nathair, disturbing them, then he raised a sandstorm around us.'

'You should have landed, attacked them on the ground,' Balor snarled.

'We did,' the grey-skinned woman said reasonably. 'But with the very air itself attacking us, what could we do? The beasts were maddened, snapping at us and at each other; we couldn't see, we couldn't even breathe. At one point, I managed to break out of the sandstorm. I spotted the one-handed boy....'

'The bard, Paedur,' the Emperor growled.

The Grey Warrior nodded. 'He was climbing onto one of the nathair. I drew my bow and prepared to fire ... and then a beast rose up before me, snatched the bow from my hands and crushed it to splinters.'

'Ragallach, the Torc Allta.'

Scathach nodded again. 'He pushed me back into the sandstorm and I lost my footing. But this is not a fight for warriors. These renegades have a powerful magician travelling with them. With the bard's cunning, the Torc Allta's strength and the northern girl's weapon skill, they are formidable indeed.'

'What do you suggest I do?' Balor demanded.

'Do not send warriors after them. Use magicians and witches to track them down. Use your own magic. Use the Earthlord's power to defeat them.' There was a knock on the door and Scathach stopped.

'Come,' Balor shouted.

The door opened and Cichal stepped into the room and bowed low before the Emperor. If he was surprised to find Scathach there before him, he didn't show it. 'I have failed you, my Emperor. I am prepared to accept my punishment.'

Balor nodded, suddenly glad to have someone to vent his anger upon. He touched the metal mask that covered half his face and then suddenly remembered that the Grey Warrior was in the room. 'You should look away, lest you too, are turned to stone.'

'Cichal is one of your most loyal and experienced warriors,' Scathach said quickly. 'Why should you punish him for your mistake?'

Cichal's tongue began flickering wildly. No-one spoke to the Emperor like that!

'If you turn him to stone all you are doing is helping your enemies. You need his battle skills. Who will replace him?'

'My mistake ... my fault?' Balor looked from Scathach to Cichal in astonishment. The Fomor stared straight ahead, saying nothing, knowing that his life was dangling by a thread.

'Cichal has failed me,' Balor said finally.

'If you sent a warrior into the icy Northlands without proper clothing and boots, would you blame him if he could not fight?' Scathach demanded.

The Emperor shook his head.

'But you sent Cichal and I against a powerful magician, even though we had no magical powers ourselves,' the Grey Warrior continued. 'Cichal never failed you in the past, but did you ever send him against magicians before?'

Balor shook his head again. Before Scathach could say another word, he raised a hand for silence and turned to Cichal. 'Did you tell this woman to say these things?'

'I did not!'

'He did not,' Scathach snapped. 'No-one tells me what to do!

Not even you,' she added, her cold grey eyes narrowing to slits.

Balor glared at the woman, the fingers of his left hand brushing his metal mask, then he suddenly turned away to the table and poured three cups of mead. 'You are right, Grey Warrior. I cannot afford to lose experienced warriors. Come let us drink together and plot the defeat of these renegades.' He passed a cup to Cichal. 'You should thank this woman, she has saved your life.'

The Fomor Officer bowed low to Scathach. 'You have saved my life, Warrior. I am in your debt. Someday, I will repay that debt. Someday, I will save your life.'

Scathach raised her cup in salute.

Balor dropped into a carved stone chair. 'Now, we need to find these renegades. Have you any idea where they are?' he looked from the woman to the Fomor.

Scathach shook her head, but Cichal said, 'I think one of them was wounded. I saw one of the red-haired human-kind being carried by the others.'

Scathach nodded in agreement. 'That's right. When we flew in over the dunes, the others were lifting the red-haired boy from a pit. Perhaps he had been hurt in the earthquake.'

Cichal finished his drink in one quick swallow. He was surprised to discover how dry his throat was. 'If he has been wounded or injured, they will need to find a healer....'

'When I last saw them they were heading west...' the Grey Warrior added.

Balor looked up suddenly. 'Do you think they will come here to Falias?' The alarm in his voice was clearly audible.

Cichal poured himself another drink. Without looking at the Emperor, he said, 'I fear so my lord. My guess is that they will come here looking for a healer.'

Balor's grip tightened on the metal cup, crushing it to scrap. 'How many healers and physicians are there in Falias,' he demanded.

'Hundreds,' Cichal said.

'Call out the guard, both Fomor and human. Seal the city; let no-one in or out. Have your warriors search the homes of all healers. And I mean every healer in the city, from the most famous to the poorest herb doctor. I want these renegades taken.' He glared at Cichal. 'If they are in Falias, I want them found, and taken!'

Ken came awake with a pounding headache and a horrible taste in his mouth. He was shocked to discover that he was lying in a narrow stone pool filled with warm water. The pool was in the centre of a round stone room which was dotted with hundreds of candles. The chamber stank of candle grease.

A bald white-bearded man appeared out of the shadows and Ken shouted with surprise, splashing wildly as he attempted to raise himself from the bath. But he was so weak he could barely lift his hands.

Paedur appeared behind the bald man, a broad smile of relief on his thin face. 'Thank the gods. You're awake.'

Ken had to swallow a couple of times before he could speak. 'What happened? Where am I?' His voice came out as little more than a harsh whisper. 'Who is this?'

'This is Diancecht,' Paedur said, perching himself on the edge of the stone pool. 'He is a healer.'

Diancecht knelt beside Paedur and touched Ken's head with his thin fingers. The boy winced. 'What are your last memories?' the healer asked.

Ken looked at the bard. Paedur nodded. 'Tell him. He has saved your life.'

'I remember I was heading down the beach looking for Ally....' He stopped. 'Ally! Where is she?'

'She's here. She's safe,' Paedur soothed him.

'What happened then?' Diancecht asked.

'The ground started to shake. I watched the sand crawling and shifting, and the water in the rock pools was shivering. And then the ground rose up all around me.' He squeezed his eyes shut and shook his head slightly. 'That's all I remember.'

'Balor used the Earthlord to destroy the Avenue of Standing Stones,' Paedur said. 'He hoped to destroy us also.'

'Ken!' They all turned as Ally raced into the room. 'You're all right!' She grabbed her brother's hand squeezing it tightly. 'He is all right?' she demanded, looking at Diancecht.

The physician nodded. 'The danger is past. He will be weak and must rest, but he will fully recover.'

Faolan and Megan came and stood behind Paedur. They had cleaned themselves up and washed their clothes and now, after a night's sleep, they felt and looked a lot better.

Paedur turned to Faolan. 'Help Ken to get dressed,' he said. Then, pushing Megan and Ally before him, he ushered Diancecht out of the room into the early morning sunlight. They stood blinking in the light, clearing the odours of wax and candle-grease out of their nostrils.

'What are you going to do now?' Diancecht asked. He stood on the edge of an ornamental pool, watching tiny red and gold fish dart quickly below the surface. He glanced sidelong at the bard. 'I mean, what are you going to do with me?'

Paedur nodded. 'You are a problem.'

'You could help us,' Ally suggested.

Diancecht smiled. 'Even if I offered, I don't think Paedur would accept my offer. Would you?'

Paedur shrugged. 'I don't think so. The Emperor has made you what you are today. You owe us nothing. I don't see why you should help us.'

The healer turned back to the still waters and nodded again. 'You're probably right.'

There was movement in the bushes and then a savage-looking creature burst out of the trees. Diancecht shouted with surprise — and fell into the pool.

Ragallach ignored him. His broad face was fixed in a grimace. 'There are Fomor coming down the street. They're headed in this direction.' He reached down with his hoof and hauled the dripping healer out of the water. His bald head was streaked with green slime. He opened his mouth to shout again, but Paedur touched him with his hook, the chill of the metal shocking him to silence.

'This is Ragallach, a Torc Allta,' the bard said quickly. 'He is with us.' Paedur looked from Ragallach to Megan. 'What are we going to do?'

The warrior maid pulled her blow-pipe from her belt. 'Fight,' she said.

The beast shook his head. 'There are too many of them. We can run or hide.' He dropped a heavy hoof onto the healer's shoulder. 'But what about our wet friend here? What are we going to do with him? We cannot leave here him....'

Diancecht shook his head from side to side. 'I will say nothing, I swear it.'

From the shadows behind them, Faolan helped Ken out into the courtyard. The red-haired boy was leaning heavily on the Windlord.

'The boy needs rest,' the healer continued. 'There are herbs and healing medicines I can give him to make him strong and well again. If you take him with you now, you will undo all that I have done for him. Leave him with me. I will look after him.'

'No!' Ally shook her head firmly. 'I'm not leaving Ken here.' She turned to Faolan. 'What about your windmagic. Could you not use it to scatter the troops?'

'I could,' he said slowly. He looked at Paedur, but the bard shook his head firmly.

'No. We need to keep all our strengths and skills to confront the Emperor.' He turned back to Diancecht. 'If I thought I could trust you, I would leave Ken and Ally here with you....'

'I give you my word as a healer,' Diancecht said quickly. 'I will not allow anything to happen to them.'

Megan reached over and squeezed the healer's plump arm. 'If anything happens to Ken or Ally, Ragallach and I will eat you.'

Paedur caught Ally's hand and drew her over to her brother. Putting his arm around Ken's waist, he supported him while they moved out of earshot of the others. The young bard's face was grim, his eyes troubled. 'I think it would be best if you two remained here with the healer,' he began.

'You cannot leave us here,' Ally blazed. 'He is the Emperor's man, you said that yourself. We'll go with you.'

'Ally,' Paedur said very softly, 'I'm not sure I can keep you safe any more. The odds are too great against us.'

'Paedur's right,' Ken said tiredly. 'If we go with the others, we risk slowing them down and maybe the lot of us will be caught. We should stay here, out of harm's way.'

'Your brother is talking sense,' the bard said. 'Diancecht won't harm you. He daren't. He's terrified of Megan and Ragallach. And he knows that Faolan's magic could tear this house down, brick by brick.'

Ally stuck her hands in her pockets. 'I still think we should have Faolan create a wind-dragon and fly us out of here.'

'And what good would that do us?' Paedur sharply. 'We would still have to get back into Falias to get close to the Emperor and the Earthlord. This time we have the element of surprise; the next time, they'll be waiting for us.'

Ken looked at Paedur. 'Take the others and go. We'll stay here. But don't forget to come and get us when you're finished.'

Paedur squeezed Ken's shoulder. 'How could we forget?'

Cichal strode down the deserted street. This was one of the wealthier parts of the city, it was quiet and respectable and nearly all the people were loyal to the Emperor.

He was looking for the home of Diancecht, healer to the Emperor, a small, stout human whom Cichal had always disliked. The man was sly and dangerous, the Fomor knew that. He pretended to be what he was not: he pretended stupidity when he was really incredibly clever. He liked people to think he was jolly and friendly, when the Fomor knew that the man often informed the Emperor about what people at court were saying and doing.

However, he was also the most important human at court and that was why Cichal himself had chosen to conduct the search of the healer's house. It would also give him a chance to break a few things. The Fomor laughed quietly; he could just imagine the look on Diancecht's face when he presented him with the warrant to search the house.

As the Fomor hammered on the front gate, Paedur and Faolan, followed by Ragallach and Megan slipped out the back. Diancecht slammed the gate after them and slid the bolts home.

'Will they be all right?' Faolan asked as the door closed.

Paedur nodded. 'They will, I'm sure of it.'

The Torc Allta bared his teeth. 'They had better be.'

They could hear the Fomor hammering on the doors on the far side of the house, and then a shout — 'Open, in the name of the Emperor.' The four companions slipped down a narrow sidestreet, keeping to the shadows. The bard paused, and looked back at the healer's house, now shining white in the early morning sunlight. He hoped Ken and Ally would be safe.

Ken lay back on a stack of rough, sweet-smelling sacks in the windowless chamber and closed his eyes.

'How can you even think about sleeping at a time like this?' Ally hissed.

'Easy. I'm tired.'

Ally prowled around the storeroom at the back of the kitchen. The floor was piled high with sacks and cotton bags filled with herbs and spices, while the walls were covered with shelves which held jugs and jars, pots, bottles and stone containers.

Something moved in the kitchen outside, pots rattled and fell to the ground, and then there was silence.

Ally held her breath. She breathed again when she heard movement overhead, heavy clumping footsteps. She sat on one of the bags beside her brother and looked at the bruising on the side of his face. Traces of the paste the healer had used were still stuck to his hair.

She suddenly realised that although they had been in danger the last time they had come to the De Danann Isle, neither of them had been hurt, and so it had all been one big adventure. This wasn't an adventure: this was real, and dangerous. Ken could have been killed. Maybe it was hopeless. After all, they were just six against the might of the Emperor's army. What could they hope to achieve? And even if they were successful and defeated Balor — what then? They had defeated him before and he had come back stronger and more dangerous than ever. Now he wanted vengeance, and he was desperate enough to send a Fomor forward through time to kill them. Wrapping her arms around herself, Ally rocked to and fro. What would have happened if their parents had been at home? She loved her mother and father dearly, they were kind and clever ... but what could they have done against a seven foot tall reptile with a stone sword? Would it have killed them too? Even the thought chilled her.

If she ever got back to her own time, she swore she was never returning here.

The house had fallen silent. Obviously, the Fomor had left.

Footsteps sounded across the stone-flagged kitchen and Ally was coming to her feet when the door opened, flooding the dimly lit storeroom with light.

'All clear,' Diancecht said.

Blinking in the sudden light, Ally helped Ken to his feet, and out into the kitchen. Diancecht slammed the door shut behind them. 'Follow me. I want Ken to bathe in the healing waters.'

Ken and Ally stepped out of the kitchen into the small courtyard — which was filled with Fomor warriors. There was movement behind them and an enormous taloned claw fell on each of their shoulders. 'We meet again,' Cichal hissed.

Ally caught hold of her brother, keeping him upright. Surprisingly, she wasn't frightened, only angry. She glared at Diancecht. 'What about your promise?' she shouted.

The healer smiled. 'Promises are made to be broken,' he said with a shrug.

Cichal bent his head and hissed, his tongue flickering, 'Diancecht the Healer is not to be trusted. But I think you know that now.'

The imperial throne room was filled with people. Fomor and human guards lined the walls, many of them armed with crossbows which were carefully trained on the prisoners standing the centre of the marbled floor.

Ally held Ken upright. Cichal had made them march from the healer's house to the palace and the trek across the city had exhausted them both, but especially Ken in his already weakened state. News of their capture had spread like wildfire across the city and the streets had been lined with silent, staring people. They thought they were coming to look at a dangerous band of renegades who had threatened the very life of the Emperor; but they were shocked to find two human children, no different from their own children except for their startling red hair and strange clothing.

As they stumbled up the broad steps of the gold-roofed palace, Ken had leaned across to his sister and whispered, 'Where are they?' He was scanning the skies, expecting Faolan to come riding in on the back of a dragon of wind and air.

'They'll be here,' Ally said with a confidence she did not feel. The Fomor were expecting a rescue attempt. There were now hundreds of the beasts surrounding them — the snake stench was incredible — and although they moved without speaking, the air was filled with the hissing rasp of their tails across the stone, the click of talons. The Fomor carried heavy-looking crossbows, which were cocked and loaded ... and most of them were pointing up into the air.

If Paedur and the others were to try to rescue them, they would be riding into a storm of metal.

The shadow of the imperial palace fell over them, and then they were marching through the high arched gate, which had been decorated with thousands of tiny pictures cut into the stone. A heavy metal gate clanged shut.

Only then did Ken and Ally finally accept that there would be no rescue.

With Cichal and Scathach on either side, Balor strode into the throne room. The humans immediately bowed deeply ... only the guards remained standing and alert, watching the courtiers and the prisoners.

The Emperor sank into his throne of polished black stone, which he had stolen from the land of the brown-skinned Toltecs. He stared hard at the two humans, the long-nailed fingers of his left hand rubbing the metal mask that covered half his face, the faint scratching sound clearly audible in the silence that had fallen over the court.

Although she was shaking inside, Ally returned Balor's stare bravely, biting the inside of her cheek to prevent herself from saying anything. Ken was slumped against her, almost asleep on his feet.

The Emperor raised his right hand. 'Make your report, Cichal.'

The Fomor bowed slightly. 'In accordance with your orders, lord, I made my way to the house of Diancecht the Healer. Because of his importance, I did not wish to insult him by having a lesser officer search his home. It took me several moments to gain entrance, which I thought unusual, though I later discovered that all the servants had been drugged. Diancecht himself opened the door. The man was nervous ... and afraid.' Cichal's tongue flickered. 'I could smell his fear.'

Balor's single eye roved over the assembled humans in the court, finally spotting the bald and bearded healer. He called him forward with a crooked finger, and then pointed, indicating that he was to stand beside the prisoners.

'First, he told me there was no-one in the house, but I could smell the scents of young human males and females, so I knew he was lying,' Cichal continued. 'When I told him this, he admitted that the renegades had been there, and that he had been forced to heal the red-haired boy, who had been injured at the Avenue of Standing Stones.'

'They made me!' Diancecht said quickly.

'He then brought the two humans out of hiding and delivered them to us,' the Fomor finished.

'They forced me,' the healer said. 'They threatened me. The northern girl said she would eat me ... and there was a beast, one of the Torc Allta — he threatened to eat me too,' he added desperately.

Balor nodded. He sat slumped in his chair, the fingers of both hands touching, fingernails gently tapping. 'You disappoint me, Diancecht,' he said eventually.

'They made me, lord....'

'Silence!' Balor thundered. 'How dare you interrupt me. You have aided my enemies. You allowed them into your home, gave them food and shelter, healed them ... and then you allowed the most dangerous to escape to continue their campaign against me!' The Emperor turned to Ally. 'Did you threaten this man?' he demanded.

'No, I did not,' she said truthfully, but then she lied, 'He helped us willingly.'

Diancecht's mouth opened and shut in shocked surprise. Like most liars he was horrified and outraged when someone lied about him.

Balor glanced sidelong at Cichal, who bent his head and hissed. 'I believe the girl. He was hiding them willingly enough; these humans had no means of threatening him. When I first arrived, he denied that they had ever been there, and he only betrayed them when I told him that I smelt them.'

Balor's teeth bared in a savage smile. 'He is a traitor, then?' he asked.

The Fomor considered a moment, then nodded. 'He has lied about this affair ... and that means he has something to hide. He betrayed these humans to us, but according to them, he helped them willingly, which means he betrayed you. Either way, he is not to be trusted.'

Balor nodded quickly. Leaning forward, he said, 'Come here, Diancecht.'

'My lord?' the healer whispered, his bald head suddenly glistening with perspiration.

The Emperor attempted a smile, but the look was savage. 'I have come to a decision. I believe your actions deserve a reward.'

The healer breathed a great sigh of relief. 'Thank you, lord.' He scurried forward, but stopped at the bottom step leading up to the throne. To his surprise the Emperor indicated that he should continue up to the very throne itself. It was an honour reserved only for the Emperor's favourites. Diancecht stared into the Emperor's face, seeing himself reflected in the metal mask. He was aware that Cichal and Scathach had stepped away, but he didn't see them waving the courtiers and guards to the ground. The Fomor guards behind Ken and Ally pushed them down.

In that instant, Ally knew what was going to happen. Although she couldn't see what was happening, she heard Balor, his voice suddenly Fomor-like, hiss, 'Receive your reward, traitor.'

Diancecht managed to say, 'No,' before his voice stopped. A dull explosion of sounds filled the court, cracking, snapping, grinding, rasping.

And then silence.

There was movement as the courtiers and Fomor guards came to the feet. Ally helped Ken upwards, and they stared in horror at what Balor had done to the healer. He had been turned into a living statue. His flesh had hardened to stone, his bald head gleaming, each individual hair on his beard was clearly outlined, his mouth open in a last terrified shout, the tip of his stone tongue protruding. Only his bright blue eyes remained alive and moving in his stone face. They were wide and darting, pleading, desperate.

Horrified, Ally realised that when Emperor turned his enemies to stone, they somehow remained alive, aware. That was the ultimate horror.

Balor came to his feet, his claws busy fixing his mask. 'Thus end all traitors.' He was turning away, when he stopped to look back at the red-haired humans. 'Take them to the dungeons. They will be executed at sunrise.'

The whispers began in the market-place, but quickly spread all over the capital.

— *Executions. Executions. Executions.*

The red-haired humans would be executed at sunrise. Only witches were executed when the sun rose, when the demons which aided them were dismissed by the light of the sun. And witches were executed by burning at the stake.

The Earthlord listened to the doors opening and closing in the distance, and then the clatter of approaching feet. He slumped tiredly in his cage. What was it to be this time? What new horror would he be forced to do for the Emperor? He had used more Earthmagic in the last few moons than he had used in his entire life. Indeed, not since the time of his grandfather, who had been one of the great Earthlords, with the ability to raise islands from the floor of the sea, had so much earth magic been used in the De Danann Isle.

He looked up from the dark water as the metal doors opened. Flickering torchlight ran off Cichal's metallic eye patch as he strode onto the river bank. The Fomor hissed in what sounded like anger. 'Why is this boy kept like this?' he demanded.

The bald jailer with the tiny red eyes shrugged and went to turn away, but the Fomor's claws tightened on his shoulder. 'Answer me!' Cichal hissed.

'He cannot,' Colum called. 'I don't believe he can speak.'

The Fomor pushed the jailer aside and crouched down on the side of the river bank, his spiked tail automatically curling around his claws. 'Why do they keep you here?'

Colum shrugged. 'I draw my Earthmagic from the soil. By keeping me in water, I cannot call up my magic.' He smiled quickly, his teeth bright in the darkness. 'Balor is a afraid that if I were free,

I would pull his palace down around him.'

The Fomor straightened. 'And would you?' he asked.

The boy nodded.

Cichal turned as the jailer pushed the two red-haired humans onto the river bank. The red-eyed man worked a lever, hauling one of the empty cages up out of the water. It dropped onto the bank, the Fomor skeleton inside rattling to pieces with the blow. Grunting, the jailer pulled open the door and tossed out the scattered bones, unceremoniously dumping them into the water.

Ally looked from the cage to the small dark-skinned boy standing knee deep in the middle of the fast flowing river. She turned to Cichal. 'You can't do this.'

'These are the Emperor's orders,' he hissed, not looking at her. He was watching the Fomor bones swirling away in the water, trying to remember the officer's name and crime.

'My brother is sick,' Ally said desperately. 'If you put him in there, he will die.'

Cichal looked up, glancing from the cage to Ken.

'He can't stand, and I can barely hold him. He will drown. And your Emperor won't like that, will he?' Ally demanded.

The Fomor shook his great head. 'No, he wants you both alive and well for your execution tomorrow.' He suddenly nodded. 'You are right, human-kind. The boy would not survive in the cage. He will be put in one of the cells. But you can go into the cage.'

Ally opened her mouth to protest, but the jailer caught her by the arm and shoved her roughly into the cage. She reached out through the bars, and caught her brother's hand, but the jailer hauled the cage high into the air, breaking their grip. The girl screamed as the cage lurched out over the river and hung suspended in the air, swinging from side to side. Ken had crawled to the side of the river bank and watched, eyes wide with horror, as his sister was slowly lowered into the river. She screamed even louder as the water washed over her feet and up to her shins. It was bitterly cold.

The jailer grabbed the back of Ken's shirt and hauled him to his feet. He was half-carried, half-dragged outside and pushed into a small windowless cell. The solid metal and stone door clanged shut, leaving him in total darkness. Too tired even to cry or shout, Ken sank to the floor, drew his knees up to his chin and rested his head on them. He couldn't hear his sister screaming any more, but that was probably because the walls were too thick. Closing his eyes he fell into a deep, dreamless sleep.

Cichal took a last look at the red-haired girl and the small dark skinned boy in cages in the middle of the river and, for the first time since he had joined the Emperor's Troop, he began to wonder if Balor wasn't mad.

Cichal was a Fomor, one of the most powerful races in the known world. They lived longer than humans, were stronger, quicker, cleverer. They had lived for a hundred generations by a powerful code of honour; when they went to war, they did not burn and loot, they fought only with other warriors and they did not attack women and children.

Cichal had lived by that code of honour. But now, he was fighting for a man — half-human, half-Fomor — who caged up children. Shaking his head, the beast turned away. Perhaps it was time to think about retiring to the Fomor Isles to grow grapes and make wine.

'I am Colum,' the small dark-skinned boy said, when the red-haired girl stopped screaming. He had never seen anyone with her hair and skin colouring. It looked as if her hair was on fire.

'I am Alison, but called me Ally, everyone else does.'

'You are one of those the Emperor fears,' the boy said quietly.

The girl didn't reply. She was attempting to climb up the bars of the cage and pull her feet out of the water. It was so cold she was beginning to lose all feeling in her toes.

'Your brother is ill?' Colum persisted.

Ally slid back into the water with a splash. Resting her head against the bars, she nodded slightly. 'He was injured when an earthquake hit the place we were staying. We got him to a healer, but he's not fully recovered yet ... not that it makes much difference,' she added bitterly. 'We are to be executed tomorrow.'

'But you had companions, did you not?' the boy asked.

Ally nodded. 'Yes...' and then she stopped. 'How did you know?'

In the flickering light of the torches, Ally could see the boy's dark face, his eyes wide and white in the gloom. 'I saw them,' he said very quietly.

'You saw them! Where? Here?'

Colum touched his forehead with his finger. 'I saw them here.' He took a deep breath and said, 'I sent the earthquake that injured your brother. I am the Earthlord.'

Ally stared at him in shock.

'I had no choice,' Colum added quickly. 'The Emperor made me.'

'How could he make you!' Ally spat. 'If you're that powerful a magician whey don't you use your magic to destroy him?'

The boy shook his head. 'It is not that simple, Ally,' he said.

'It is,' she snapped.

'No,' he continued. 'He keeps me here in this running water so that I cannot call up my power.' He took a deep breath and added. 'And he is holding my mother and my younger brother and sister prisoner on the Fomor Isles. If I don't do as he says, he will have the Fomor eat them.' His voice had fallen to a terrified whisper. 'So you see, Ally, there is nothing I can do.'

Balor leaned on the windowsill and stared down over the city. The long hot day was slipping into night, and the sky to the east was already dark with stars, which mirrored the countless fires burning in the streets and alleys below. 'Will they come?' he asked, without turning around.

Scathach knelt before the huge fire, her stone grey eyes closed, the firelight running off her sharply filed teeth. The heat eased away the pain and stiffness of her many old injuries.

'Will the bard, the Windlord and the others come?' Balor snapped.

Scathach nodded without opening her eyes. 'They will come,' she said simply. 'This young bard has been trained in the old ways, he is honourable. The Windlord is in debt to the bard and will follow him. The Torc Allta ...' she shrugged. 'Who knows what one of the boar-folk think? The warrior maid will follow because she has nothing else to do.' A smile twisted the woman's hard face. 'I understand that.'

'When will they attack? Tonight?'

'I don't think so. The Torc Allta would be in his pig shape; they would not have the advantage of his great strength.'

Balor swung around from the window. The human half of his face was in shadow, but the metal mask glowed red and gold with the firelight. 'In the morning then?'

The Grey Warrior nodded. 'That is when I would attack. The Windlord will probably rise a storm, the beast and the warrior maid will attack our troops, and the bard will free the humans.'

Balor began to laugh, a chill hissing sound.

'Something amuses you, my lord?'

'Even now, I have gathered together a dozen of my most powerful magicians. In the chamber below us they are creating a magical shield which they will set over Falias. If the Windlord uses his windmagic, the spell will rebound back upon him. It will probably tear him and his companions to pieces!'

Scathach threw back her head and joined in the laughter. In the corridor beyond, Cichal, who had listened to every word, moved away when he heard the chilling laughter. What Balor hadn't told the Warrior Woman was that not one of the those twelve magicians who were creating and maintaining the magical shield would be alive when the day was out. The effort of creating the shield and keeping it over a city as large as Falias would have withered and aged them.

Deep in the heart of the poorest part of the city, Paedur and Faolan watched while Megan slipped into the dark foul-smelling waters of the open sewer. Ragallach in his pig-shape bobbed beside her.

'I hope you're sure about this,' she hissed at Paedur.

'I'm sure,' Paedur said confidently.

Megan nodded and released the side of the bank. She was immediately pulled away by the current.

'Are you sure?' Faolan asked quietly.

'No,' Paedur said simply. He watched the two figures disappear into the darkness.

'Then why did you let them go?'

'What other choice did we have?' Paedur asked simply.

'We have my magic!'

'Balor knows we're here. He knows about your magic. You can be sure he's taken precautions.' The bard paused and added, 'The type of precautions that could kill you.' He reached out and squeezed Faolan's arm. 'Come, we've a lot to do before the dawn.'

'I am the Earthlord,' Colum said, his voice echoing slightly in the underground cavern. He turned in the cage, gripping the bars as the tug of rushing water threatened to pull him over. 'My grandfather was the one of the Lords of the Elements, the last of the great Earthlords. Growing tired of his life at court, he moved away and settled in a tiny village to the south-east of here.'

Ally nodded. She was so cold that she could barely concentrate on what the small boy was saying. Although he looked no more than seven, she guessed that he was much older. Perhaps his race were like the African pygmies.

'We live close to the swamplands and the air is not good there, especially during the hot summer months. My father died of the fever when I was very young and so my grandfather trained me in the Elemental magic before he too died. I used my magic for simple things: building dams, making caves, altering the course of rivers to irrigate our fields, raising walls of stone and mud. We were a simple people, leading simple lives. And we were happy.'

'Until Balor came?' Ally guessed.

The boy nodded. 'They came with the dawn, streaming out of the sky, hundreds of Fomor on nathair. We could not fight them. We only had a few crude weapons — spears, wooden swords and knives — and what good would they have been against the armour and scales of the Fomor? And we are not a tall race — only the red-haired Small Folk are smaller than us — and the Fomor were like giants to us. More than half of their number landed and surrounded the village, while the rest remained in the sky, circling overhead, their ugly shadows rippling across the ground. The serpent-folk gathered together every man, woman and child. Then Balor appeared, riding out of the sky on a enormous white nathair with blazing red eyes.' He squeezed his eyes shut, remembering the terrifying creature. 'I've seen red, gold, brown and the fierce black nathair. I've never seen a white one before.'

'An albino,' Ally said, her teeth chattering with the cold. She wanted Colum to stop talking so she could close her eyes and sleep. But she was afraid that if she slept, she might slip beneath the water and drown. 'An albino is a creature without colour,' she explained.

Colum nodded. 'The Emperor asked for the Earthlord and his family. No-one moved. I was standing with my mother, brother and sister with the rest of the villagers. But no one betrayed us.

' "I will destroy the village," Balor said. But still no-one moved. Then Balor said that he would kill all the old people in the village. We didn't believe him ... until he sent his creatures into our midst and they began picking out the elders.

'I knew then it was useless.

'I thought about using my Earthmagic, about opening a great pit beneath Balor and his Fomor, but I knew that many of our own people would die also.

' "I want the Earthlord and his family," Balor said.

'So we came forward, my mother carrying my sister, I holding my younger brother's hand. For a moment I though that the Emperor didn't believe us, didn't believe that I was the Earthlord. Then he stretched out his hand and held it over my head.

' "You are the Earthlord," he said. "I can feel the power flowing from you."

'What do you want? I asked.

' "I want you to serve me," Balor said.

'I shook my head. Never.

'But Balor snapped his fingers and my mother, sister and brother were caught up by the Fomor and bundled onto a nathair. Without a sound it rose up into the sky and then immediately set off to the south.

'Where are you taking them? I asked.

'Balor's grin was terrifying. "To the Fomor Isles," he said. "They will ensure your good behaviour. If you do as I say, then they will remain unharmed. But the day you disobey me, then that is the day I will allow the Fomor to eat them." '

Ally gasped in horror. 'They wouldn't!'

Colum nodded. 'They would. The Fomor look on us humans as cattle. They will kill and eat us in the same way that we eat cows or pigs. In the human cities, the Fomor eat our food, but there are still said to be places where human meat is served.'

Ally swallowed hard. 'That's disgusting.'

Colum shrugged. 'Meat is meat.'

'I think I'll become a vegetarian,' Ally muttered.

'A what?'

'A vegetarian. Someone who does not eat meat.'

The boy's teeth flashed in a quick smile. 'I think it's a bit late now to be coming to that decision.'

'Is there anything we can do?' the girl asked.

'What can I do?' Colum said bitterly. 'I possess enough power to destroy Balor and this entire city ... and yet I cannot use it, because it will put my family's life in danger.' A note of anger crept into his voice. 'Balor has used me to bring victory to his army. He's forced me to call up my magic to destroy cities, burst dams, flood towns and villages.' He stopped and took a deep breath. 'He's made me abuse my power.'

'It wasn't your fault. You are not to blame.'

'But I am to blame for all those people who died or were injured when I made the earth quake and shiver beneath them. I made it happen.'

'You were forced to make it happen!' Ally said firmly.

Colum fell silent. He rested his head against the bars and attempted to call up a little of his power, concentrating hard to feel the earth beneath the water. A tingle of warmth flowed into him. 'Give me your hand,' he said, stretching his arm through the bars.

Ally pressed herself against the bars and stretched out her hand. Her fingertips brushed the boy's hand.

The Earthlord felt the power of the soil flow up through his body and out along his outstretched arm...

...and Ally shuddered when the warmth suddenly flooded through her body, tingling in her numb feet and toes.

Colum sagged against the bars, breaking contact with the girl. His dark-skinned face was sheened with sweat and he was breathing deeply. 'I'm sorry I cannot do more. The water acts as a barrier which prevents me from calling upon my power.'

'Why hasn't Balor taken your power?' Ally asked.

'Elemental magic is not like other magic, which any magician can master. Only the Lords of the Elemental Magic can control their particular element, earth, air, fire or water. The power is passed on from generation to generation, from father to son, mother to daughter. Balor cannot control our magic, but he can control us.'

Ally shook the bars of the cage. 'Is there no way out of here?'

Colum shook his head. 'Not for me. I must do as he says.'

'What is going to happen to Ken and I?' she asked suddenly.

'What exactly did the Emperor say?'

'He said we would be executed at sunrise.'

The boy closed his eyes, shaking his head. 'Then you will be burnt at the stake.' He paused, allowing himself to become aware of the rhythm of the earth around him. 'Even now the sky is lightening towards the dawn. The sun will rise within a few moments.'

Had the night gone so quickly? Ally felt sudden tears sting her eyes.

Overhead, a door clanged open and shut, and metal-tipped boots sounded on the stone floor.

'I'm sorry, Ally,' Colum whispered. 'Truly, I am sorry.'

Ken came awake as the cell door slammed open. Before he was fully awake he was hauled outside by the huge bald jailer. A Fomor officer caught him by the arm. Ken felt completely rested after his night's sleep. His drowsiness had passed and he was alert and refreshed. He stared at the Fomor: there was something familiar about him, about the pattern of scales around his yellow eyes.

Looking past the serpent, Ken saw the fat jailer open the second door and step down onto the river bank. He could see the cages in the water and, although it was dim, he spotted Ally's red hair. The cages were supported by chains, which were connected to a series of pulleys in the roof, and which ended in thick wheels set into the floor. The bald man turned a massive handle and, using his great strength, began to haul in Ally's cage.

Ken looked at the Fomor again. 'I know you,' he said suddenly. 'You chased Ally and myself through our house!'

The beast seemed startled, then he slowly nodded. 'I am Goll,' he hissed. 'I was sent to bring back your heads. I failed in my duty because of you. I asked to be allowed to bring you to your doom.'

The cage dropped to the ground with a clang of metal. The jailer opened the heavy square padlock and pulled back the door. Ally screamed as she was roughly hauled out.

'You are to be burnt at the stake,' the Fomor continued. 'And I have also been given the honour of lighting the fire beneath you.'

Ken was about to reply, but then he saw what was happening behind the beast on the riverbank.

He saw Megan rise up out of the dark water, her blow-pipe already to her lips. He saw the red-eyed jailer clutch at his throat, and then slowly topple forwards into the fast flowing water.

He saw the small pink pig — looking like a skinny dog with its hair plastered to its body — hop up onto the river bank. It stopped, shuddering ... and then it changed. It grew. Bones stretched, muscles elongated and filled out, ribs curled, the plates of its skull altered, its tusks growing to wicked points, its face taking on an almost human-like appearance. Even though Ken had seen the were-change often, it still terrified him. Ragallach the Torc Allta rose to his feet.

Goll leaned forward and hissed. 'I think I will enjoy watching you roast.'

Suddenly the Fomor was swept up in the air, massive arms holding him high. The beast scrabbled for his sword, but it slipped from its scabbard and clattered to the floor.

Ragallach bounced the Fomor off the ceiling and caught him as he fell. Holding the struggling serpent over his head, he ducked back through the door again. With an enormous effort, he tossed Goll out into the middle of the river. The Fomor struck in an explosion of water and mud. He managed to scream out once before he was swept away into the darkness.

Megan and Ally joined Ken and Ragallach. 'You didn't think we'd leave you, did you?' the Torc Allta demanded.

'I know you wouldn't,' Ally said softly, but then her voice changed, becoming harder, sharper. 'But what kept you so long!'

'I cannot come with you,' Colum said sadly when Ragallach had hauled his cage to the shore and snapped off the lock.

'His family are being held prisoner on the Fomor Islands,' Ally said quickly. 'If he leaves with us, the Emperor will order them eaten.'

'He wouldn't do that,' Ken said quickly.

Megan squeezed water from her thick hair and nodded. 'He would.'

'Look, you must go,' Colum said urgently. 'They will be wondering what has happened.'

Ragallach looked at the small boy. 'You have the power to defeat Balor,' he grunted.

'But I cannot use it.'

'If your family were free though, would you be able to defeat Balor?' the Torc Allta persisted.

'Of course. But....'

Ragallach held up a paw. 'We will find your family. We will rescue them. Then together, you and the Windlord can destroy this evil Emperor. Yes?' he asked.

Colum nodded. 'Yes. Yes, of course. But how?'

Ragallach rose to his feet. 'We will return with your family,' he promised. 'But first we have to get out of here.'

'Paedur said to give him a sign if we broke free,' Megan reminded him.

'Then let me help you,' the Earthlord said quickly.

Ally shook her head. 'You'll only get into trouble with the Emperor.'

The boy smiled. 'I'll say you forced me to help you.'

Balor shifted uneasily in his seat in the middle of the open square before the palace. The impressive throne had been a gift from the people of Falias. A dozen different woods had been worked into it, polished, carved and etched to create a masterpiece of the carver and woodworker's art. It was truly a throne fit for a king. But Balor hated it. He hated sitting on it; it was the most uncomfortable piece he possessed. All of Balor's furniture was specially imported from the Fomor Isles or crafted by Fomor carpenters ... because Fomor craftsmen created chairs for creatures with tails.

And one of Balor's most closely guarded secrets was that he possessed a stub of a tail at the end of his spine.

'Where are they?' the Emperor demanded, surging to his feet once again, turning to look back towards the palace.

'They will be here, lord,' Scathach said slowly. She was watching the final pieces of wood being added to the two huge stacks that had been erected in the centre of the square.

But Cichal, who had taken up his usual position behind the Emperor's throne was also becoming uneasy. He had allowed his own hatchling, Goll to collect the prisoners; he didn't want any mistakes. They should have been here by now. Unless something had gone wrong. 'Perhaps I should go and see what is causing the delay...' he began, and then stopped.

The two tall pyramids of dry wood were slowly falling apart, logs rolling off the pile onto the ground. A section of the nearest stack collapsed inwards ... and the whole, carefully constructed pile broke up, the thick oil-covered logs rolling to the foot of the Emperor's chair.

Cichal felt it then: a tremor in the air like distant thunder. His tongue flickered madly, tasting the air, but there was no scent of rain — and then he realised that it was the very air itself that was vibrating!

The Fomor crouched down on all fours, resting his long claws on the flagstones, feeling the vibrations trembling up through his nails. 'It's coming from below,' he hissed.

The trembling increased.

Balor looked down at Cichal, a frown on his half-face. 'An earthquake..?' he asked, and then comprehension dawned in his single green eye. 'The Earthlord! But how?'

The ground erupted in two solid columns of rock, showering mud and soil and broken stones across the square. The pillars of stone swayed from side to side for a few moments, before they crashed down across the square.

The screams of the assembled crowd were drowned out as a series of ragged cracks ran across the smoothly paved square. Then the paving stones began to explode upwards, punched up from beneath and tossed high into the sky as if they were weightless. They fell and shattered on the stones with a series of terrific cracks. All across the square the stones were vibrating madly, some of them shivering to grey powder, or crumbling underfoot when people ran across them.

Balor leapt from his wooden throne with a roar of rage and fear as the paving stones around him began to tremble violently. He watched in horror as a heavy stone directly beneath the throne exploded up through the seat, reducing it to matchwood. Splinters circled in the air, raining down on Balor. The Emperor turned to look for his guards but, with the exception of Cichal and Scathach, they had all run off, terrified as the stones beneath their feet attacked them. Scathach lay on the ground, fingers dug into the exposed earth, desperately attempting to hang on as the earth heaved like a ship at sea. Cichal stood with his legs apart, using his tail to give him extra support.

'Earthmagic,' Balor howled. 'Get down to the dungeons. 'Stop him,' he roared above the sounds of grinding rock and snapping stone. 'Don't let the humans escape.'

But Cichal shook his head. He pointed over Balor's shoulder. 'Too late,' he cried.

Balor turned. A huge pit had opened up in the centre of the square. The sides were as smooth as if they had been cut with a knife. Smoke and dust curled up from the middle of the pit.

And in the centre of the pit an almost circular column of stone was slowly growing upwards. There were figures lying on the flat surface of the stone; they were all coated in grey dust so it was impossible to make out their features, but there was a Torc Allta amongst the group.

'Archers ... archers!' Balor screamed. He grabbed Cichal by the shoulder and pushed him towards the pit. 'Get them. Don't let them get away.'

The Fomor Officer pulled his sword free and moved quickly across the broken ground. He was measuring the distance between the edge of the pit and island of stone the humans were on. He thought he might be able to make it with a leap ... if he missed though, he would fall straight into the dungeons.

The island of stone stopped moving and the trembling in the ground died away. In the centre of the pillar of stone, Colum could barely keep his tired eyes open. 'I've done all I can. I can do no more.'

Ally was still blinking dust from her eyes. She had already seen magic worked on the De Danann Isle, but she had never experienced such raw power before. First, the Earthlord had opened an enormous hole in the roof of the dungeon, and then he had actually made the earth they were standing on move upwards, like a flower growing towards the light. It had been a terrifying experience.

Ken pointed to the black-coated crossbowmen running down from the palace and out of the alleyways. 'I think we're in trouble.'

'Where are Paedur and Faolan?' Megan muttered, slipping a dart into her blowpipe.

Cichal strode to the edge of the pit and looked across the gap that separated him from the humans and Torc Allta. 'You made a brave effort,' he hissed. 'But in the end, it was a wasted effort. You have nowhere to go. Surrender to me now, before the Emperor orders his archers to cut you down.'

Ally shook Colum's shoulder. 'There must be something you can do?'

The Earthlord slumped against her, eyes flickering. 'I'm tired, so tired.'

'The effort of calling up the magic has exhausted him,' Ragallach said gently.

'What are we going to do then?' Ally asked desperately.

Megan glanced back over her shoulder, her dark eyes shining. 'We can fight, or we can surrender.'

More and more archers were surrounding the pit now, crossbows and bows pointing at the four humans and the Torc Allta.

Ragallach grunted. 'If we surrender, we have the chance of fighting again,' he said slowly.

'But where's Paedur,' Ken asked. 'I thought you said he was waiting for your signal.'

'Maybe something's happened,' Ragallach said very softly.

'Surrender,' Cichal called.

'Never,' the Torc Allta shouted.

Balor staggered to the edge of the pit. His fine clothes were soiled and torn, his metal face mask streaked with dirt. The human half of his face was crimson with rage. 'Kill them,' he screamed. 'Kill them! Kill them all!'

Ragallach rose to his feet, his huge arms raised high. 'We surrender.'

The Emperor was almost dancing with rage. 'Too late for that,' he screamed. 'Kill them now!'

The archers drew back their bows.

Ghost white, crimson-eyed, the albino nathair, wings and claws extended crashed into Balor and Cichal, pitching them out over the edge of the pit. Their hissing screams ended as they fell into the river far below. The nathair's taloned wings swept another dozen archers and crossbowmen off the edge of the pit as it came in to land on the pillar of stone.

Paedur slid down off the back of the enormous flying serpent, and hauled Ally to her feet. 'Get on, quickly,' he shouted, almost throwing her onto the creature's back. Faolan leaned down and hauled her up into the saddle behind him.

Megan flashed a quick grin at the young bard as she ran past and vaulted onto the nathair's back. 'That was very close.'

'Closer than you'll ever realise,' Paedur shouted.

Ken was kneeling on the ground staring up at the creature. 'I ... I can't,' he stuttered.

Paedur suddenly remembered the boy's fear of flying reptiles. Catching Ken's chin, forcing his head up, Paedur used his specially trained storyteller's voice to hypnotise the boy. Staring deep into his eyes, he spoke in a deep, almost melodic voice. 'You will come with me. You will not fear the nathair.' Ken's eyes blinked, then lost all expression.

'I'll take care of him,' Ragallach said, lifting the hypnotised boy in his arm and passing him up to Megan and Ally. He nodded to the Earthlord. 'He cannot come with us, though he has saved our lives. Balor holds his family captive on the Fomor Isles.'

Paedur went and knelt by the Earthlord. Colum was struggling to keep his eyes open and beneath his deeply tanned skin, he looked pale. His eyes seemed far too big for his face. 'Free my family,' he said urgently, clutching at Paedur's cloak. 'Free them ... and I can destroy the Emperor. Promise me.'

Paedur pressed the first two fingers of his right hand to the bardic badge high on his left shoulder. 'I will free your family. I swear it on my honour as a bard.'

'Paedur,' Ragallach suddenly bellowed, 'the archers are regrouping.'

The bard raced across the island of stone and vaulted onto the nathair's bony back even as the first arrows were whistling through the air. 'Up, up,' he shouted.

Faolan worked the reins, allowing a little light to flash through the top of the nathair's hood. The creature's great body coiled, then its muscles worked, pushing it upwards. Its enormous wings snapped open, catching the air. Arrows hissed in from all sides. Some actually struck the nathair, but they couldn't penetrate its scales. The nathair circled up on the crisp dawn air, riding towards the light.

'Where to?' Faolan shouted.

Paedur, who had been staring down at the devastation that the Earthlord had wreaked in the centre of Falias, pointed off to the right. 'South. We fly for the Fomor Isles.'

'We knew we couldn't use Faolan's windmagic to rescue you,' Paedur shouted above the roar of the wind, 'the Emperor would have been expecting that. So we did what he least expected us to do.'

'What was that?' Ally asked.

Faolan twisted in the high wooden saddle and looked back at her. 'We crept into the palace!'

'That's not entirely true,' Paedur said, with a quick smile. 'We crept into the palace grounds, and made our way to the stables.'

Ragallach grunted. 'You walked through the palace grounds?' he said in disbelief. 'But surely it was swarming with guards.'

Paedur nodded. 'But they were all looking up, expecting trouble from the skies.'

'They were expecting a wind dragon or a storm,' Faolan laughed.

The bard slapped the scaly serpent beneath them. 'In the nathair nests, we found this creature. I kept watch while Faolan saddled and hooded it. And then we waited for your signal.'

Faolan laughed again. 'I wasn't sure what I was waiting for,' he said, 'but I certainly wasn't expecting such a spectacular exit.'

'Ragallach and Megan saved us just in time,' Ally said. 'The guards were just taking us out of the cells when they arrived.' She looked at Megan, who was lying alongside her, holding tightly to the side of the saddle. 'How did you find us?'

The warrior maid smiled shyly. 'It wasn't easy. We knew about the stream that flowed beneath the palace, and Paedur had heard about the cages that hung over the water....'

'*In* the water,' Ally said quickly, shivering with the thought of the biting, numbing cold.

'We spent the night wandering through the sewers of Falias looking for that stream. As the night wore on and there was no sign of it, we became quite desperate. We came out into what looked like a huge circular room, and all around us, set high up and low down on the walls were at least twenty pipes, all of them dripping water into the circular chamber. Ragallach went from pipe to pipe, smelling and tasting the difference in the water, until he finally chose one particular pipe.' She paused and added quietly. 'I knew it was getting close to the dawn. I didn't think we were going to make it, but Ragallach kept pushing along. We were going against the water and the effort was exhausting, but it must have been doubly so for a small pig.'

Ally nodded. She looked out over Faolan's shoulder, and felt sudden tears sting her eyes. They had all risked so much to help Ken and herself.

The Windlord felt moisture splash onto his cheek and turned his head, strands of his golden hair flying back into Ally's face. 'Why do you weep?' he asked, the wind whipping away his words.

She shook her head. 'I don't know. Because of what you all did,' she said slowly. 'You could have left us there. My brother and I cannot help you in this quest — in fact, so far we've only hindered you. But you came for us.'

Faolan looked puzzled. 'Are we not friends?'

Ally nodded. 'I'd like to think so.'

'And if we had let you die, what sort of friends would we have been?' he asked. 'There is an ancient saying on the De Danann Isle: "Man is born without choice into a family. Friends are chosen."'

'There is a similar saying in my time.'

'We are friends,' Faolan said simply.

Ally nodded silently, turning her head to look from Faolan to Paedur, then at Ragallach and Megan and even her own brother. She was turning back to Faolan when she spotted movement in the clouds behind them. She squinted, then pointed, 'Nathair!' she screamed.

Scathach led the nathair, riding a night-black serpent with enormous yellow eyes. She hadn't waited to see what had become of Balor and Cichal. When the albino nathair had slammed into them, she had turned and raced back to the palace. There was confusion in the stables as Fomor and human troops milled about, wondering what to do. Rumours of the Emperor's death were already beginning to circulate. Scathach had run into the stables and demanded that the nathair be saddled for immediate flight. A Fomor warrior attempted to argue with her, but Scathach's twin swords flashed out, coming to rest on either side of the serpent's throat. The Fomor stared into the woman's stone-grey eyes and realised that she meant it. 'Prepare the black nathair,' he had called, without turning around.

While the white nathair was still visible in the sky to the south of Falias, twenty of the fierce black war-nathair took to the air. The young Fomor riders — chosen because their light weight would enable the serpents to fly further — wore no armour and carried curved hunting bows and the powerful Fomor crossbows. Each beast carried a quiver of forty arrows; they were all excellent shots.

Scathach's narrow face was expressionless as she quickly caught up with the humans on the heavily laden white nathair. She hadn't understood Cichal's fear of this small renegade band, but she did now, and she realised that if they weren't stopped, they would topple the Emperor ... and the Grey Warrior didn't want that. Not just yet anyway. She had plans of her own for Balor. Before the year turned, she intended to be the Empress of the De Danann Isles. And nothing was going to stand in her way.

'We'll never outrun them,' Faolan said. 'Their nathair are faster and carrying less weight.'

Paedur looked up into the clear blue sky. It was cloudless. Looking behind him, he saw that the nathair were closer now. His sharp eyesight made out the figure of Scathach on the lead serpent.

'We've got to go down,' he said. 'We'll land and try to lose them.'
He leaned over the edge of the nathair's white body and looked at
the land far below. All he could see were the tops of thick trees,
occasionally cut through with twisting bands of rivers. The sea was
a blue line in the distance and he could just about make out the haze
of the Fomor Isles.

There was a long whistling scream, and then a hollow headed
arrow flashed overhead.

All thoughts of reaching the islands faded as more and more
arrows began to whistle around them. The black nathair grew ever
closer. Some had even started to pull ahead. Another arrow plunged
deep into the wooden saddle, directly in front of Ally. She stared at
the vibrating shaft in horror. An inch to either side and it would have
gone straight through her.

They were almost surrounded: nathair on either side, others
above them. They heard Scathach's screaming war cry carried on
the wind. It sounded like the cry of a creature in pain.

'Down Faolan, down!' Paedur shouted desperately.

Faolan dropped the hood over the creature's eyes, completely
blinding it. It immediately folded its wings and dropped like a stone.
The humans' screams and the Torc Allta's squeals were drowned
as arrows and crossbow shafts sliced through the air.

The black nathair whirled in confusion before they followed the
falling creature, firing shot after shot. Scathach smiled triumphantly. She had them now. They would either be shot out of the
air, or they would crash into the jungle below. Either way, they were
dead.

The white nathair's massive wings snapped open and beat, beat and beat again, brushing the tops of the tall trees, scattering leaves and snapping twigs as it attempted to remain in the air.

Two of the black nathair, who had followed too closely behind, were startled by the sudden appearance of the huge white wings. Their own wings lost rhythm and they crashed onto the treetops where they hung for a few moments, before tumbling to the ground far below.

A third Fomor, seeing what had happened to his companions, brought his nathair in at a different angle, coming at the renegades from behind. He had notched an arrow to his bow when he saw the dark-haired female sit up on the back of the beast and look at him. He saw her put a tube to her lips. He felt the pin-prick beneath his chin. His claws touched a feathered dart in his neck....

The Fomor went cartwheeling back off the nathair and crashed into the trees. The riderless nathair rose upwards, spiralling towards the light.

It took all of Faolan's skill and strength to bring the albino nathair around. It was hissing madly, its great mouth opening and closing. It could feel the trees brushing its belly, flapping against its wings, and it wanted to rise higher.

Paedur tapped Faolan on the shoulder and pointed. 'There!' he shouted.

Faolan brought the nathair down into a small clearing in the heart of the jungle. As soon as the beast had touched the ground, Ragallach, Paedur and Megan leaped off. While Megan watched the skies above, her blow-pipe to her lips, Ragallach lifted the still-sleeping Ken off the nathair's back and Ally and Faolan slid to the ground. Paedur cut the nathair's reins with his hook and then slapped its rump with the flat of his metal hook. The creature took to the air with an angry hissing.

'Run,' Ragallach shouted, grabbing Ken and throwing him over his shoulder, as the first of the nathair flew over the clearing. Arrows began buzzing and screaming into the soft earth. Two of the Fomor jerked from their saddles as Megan's darts struck home. One of the beasts fell to the ground, while the second became entangled in his saddle and hung to one side, causing the nathair to circle round and around.

Once into the shelter of the trees, Paedur caught Faolan by the arm. 'Windlord, you must use your power now!'

'But Balor will know where we are!' Faolan protested.

Paedur nodded to the fifteen remaining nathair that were coming in to land. 'If they catch up with us, it won't matter!'

'I'll need your strength,' Faolan said.

Paedur took up position behind the Windlord, placing his hand on the centre of the boy's back and allowing a little of his own strength to flow from him. He felt Faolan straighten with the surge of energy.

The Windlord closed his eyes and breathed deeply, tasting the rich soup of jungle odours, then slowly, slowly, he began to call on the ancient windlore. He knew that to work a spell like this he really needed time and preparation, but there simply was no time. He could feel the warm glow of the bard's strength flowing into him. The spell would have to be something simple he decided as he stretched out his hands and threw his head back. He felt the currents of air on his face, crawling across his skin, tingling in his fingertips. There were fifteen nathair, and the flying serpents were nervous creatures.

A smile touched the boy's lips.

The Windlord slowly brought his hands around in front of his body, pressing them together, feeling the resistance as an invisible ball of air gathered in his palms. He shaped the wind, working it with his fingers, rolling it on his palms.

Paedur looked over his shoulder and saw the boy's hands moving. Although he could see nothing, the energy in the air sent tingles into his hook.

Faolan moved his right hand, drew it back and then forward, as if he was throwing a stone.

Paedur squinted, barely able to make out a vague disturbance in the air, like a heat haze, but concentrated into a fist-sized ball. The ball flew into the midst of the nathair.

There was a terrific explosion, a flat detonation of sound that terrified nathair and Fomor alike. A second and third explosion followed as Faolan threw two more of the invisible airballs in among the creatures. The explosions brought the treetops alive with countless thousands of birds. They rose wheeling and cawing into the sky, surrounding the terrified flying serpents, completely confusing them. Some of the birds, obviously fearing that their treetop nests were under threat, attacked the nathair and Fomor with beaks and claws.

Faolan sagged and the bard caught him. The Windlord's eyes were heavy with exhaustion. 'How was that?' he asked.

'Perfect,' the bard said. 'But what did you do?'

'Bags of air,' Faolan said simply. 'Just bags of air. When they burst, they bang.'

The bard helped Faolan through the tangled undergrowth, to where the others were crouching, out of sight of the Fomor archers. Ken was unmoving, his eyes wide and staring, still under the bard's hypnotic spell. Paedur touched the side of his face with his hook, and the boy jerked awake. He looked around in confusion. Ally drew him to one side, 'I'll tell you what happened,' she said with a smile. 'You really will have to get over your fear of snakes.'

Paedur crouched down on the soft ground, clearing a patch with the edge of his hook. Faolan slumped to the forest floor, with his back to a tree, exhausted by the effort of calling the wind, while Megan and Ragallach took up a position on either side of the bard. With the point of his hook, Paedur sketched the outline of the coast, then two larger islands and a group of six smaller islands.

'We are somewhere here,' he said, tapping the ground with a twig. 'This is the Forest of Caesir. It is supposed to cover the Heart of the World. It is said that if a man were to travel to the lands across the sea, either to the west or east, to the lands of the copper-skins or the black-skins, then one would find a continuation of this forest.'

'Amongst my people,' Ragallach said slowly, 'there is a myth that in the beginning there was only one land surrounded by water. But then the gods fought and the land was split and torn asunder, creating the islands.'

Paedur nodded. 'I know the legend. Perhaps it is true — all

legends have at least a grain of truth in them. And it is certainly interesting that these trees and many of the animals that inhabit this forest can also be found on the neighbouring islands.' The bard touched the larger of the two islands with the twig. 'The majority of the Fomor live on these two islands in caves deep beneath the earth.' He smiled quickly. 'Don't forget, they have serpent blood in them, and snakes prefer cool caverns. There are very few buildings on the surface of the island, though the islands themselves are very carefully cultivated; the Fomor grow grapes, and the wine they produce is considered the finest in the known world.'

'I suppose these islands are well guarded?' Megan asked.

Paedur shook his head. 'Surprisingly not. After all, who is going to attack the savage Fomor? Also, there is nothing on the island to attract an invader. The Fomor live simple lives, growing their grapes and the few grains they use. They fish, hunt on the islands and here, on the mainland. They have no interest in precious metals, preferring to work in stone. Getting onto the island will not be a problem. Getting off will.'

Ragallach looked at the map. 'Where do you think we will we find the Earthlord's family?'

'Probably here.' Paedur pointed to the bigger of the two islands. 'Morc rules the Fomor Isles from an underground palace. If the Emperor was sending Colum's family away for safekeeping, that's where he would have sent them.'

A smile touched Megan's lips. 'Will they be expecting us?'

'Probably,' Paedur muttered.

Scathach finally reached the bottom of the enormously tall tree close to noon. The Grey Warrior was bleeding from dozens of scratches, there was a bruise on her right cheekbone, and one of her front teeth felt loose.

One of the Windlord's explosions had detonated almost on top of her. The sudden sound had shocked her motionless, while her black nathair had twisted with fright. The saddle girths had snapped with the violent movement and Scathach was catapulted from the saddle. She didn't know how far she had fallen — it felt like a long way, though she knew she had been flying just above the level of the trees. She had crashed onto the treetops, toppled, tumbled, fell, bouncing from branch to branch before she managed to grab a handful of twigs and hold on.

It had taken her most of the morning to make her way to the ground. The tree was alive with birds of all shapes and sizes, and once a bird with blood-red feathers had jumped out at her screaming madly, almost knocking her to the ground with the shock. But there were other, even more dangerous creatures in the tree. She encountered snakes several times. Some were enormous fat-bodied creatures, with dull-coloured scales that blended into the background, others were tiny, brightly coloured, and deadly. It was only as she neared the bottom of the tree that she became aware of the other creatures that lived in the branches: small, man-like creatures, completely covered in hair, with long twisting tails. These were the Simpean-sai, creatures of legend. They were neither man nor true beast, nor were they part of the were-folk, though they were similar to the hugely powerful Gor Allta, who also inhabited these forests. They watched her with black shining eyes. She didn't think they were dangerous, but she still loosened her dagger in its sheath.

Scathach fell once, a rotten branch giving way beneath her, dropping her hard onto a twisted mass of branches, which held her weight for a moment, before they too snapped and she fell again. Dragging her knife free she plunged it deep into the tree trunk and held on. The sudden jerk almost wrenched her shoulders from their sockets. Hauling herself upright, she sat on a branch and calmed her breathing. When she looked down she discovered that she was a short way from the ground.

When Scathach finally dropped to the ground, she knelt on the soft damp earth and closed her eyes, praying to her savage northern gods. These renegades had humiliated her, defeated her, left her marooned and stranded in this wild place. Scathach called upon Hiisi, the Lord of Evil and Kalma, the Goddess of Death and Tuoni the God of the Underworld, begging their help, promising them the souls of the renegades.

When she straightened, her face was a vicious mask. She was no longer content to kill them, now she would condemn them to everlasting torment in the Otherworld.

Pulling her two swords free, the Grey Warrior set off in pursuit of the humans and the Torc Allta.

The jungle came alive at night.

It was noisy during the day, but when the sun sank, the noise level increased: roars, shouts, whoops, high-pitched jittering laughter and deep coughing growls echoed through the darkness.

They had spent the day moving deeper into the jungle, gnawing on roots and eating berries which Ragallach, with his animal-like senses had pronounced safe.

As evening fell, Paedur had gathered everyone into a clearing. While Ragallach and Megan cut branches from thick thorn trees to form a protective circle around them, he had lit a fire in the centre of the clearing. 'This fire must be kept going all night,' he said, 'so we will have to sleep in shifts.' He stopped, staring at Ragallach who was looking up into the purple sky.

'The sun is about to sink,' the beast said. 'I can feel it.' He looked at his companions, his bright pink eyes startling against the darkness. 'When I take on my animal shape, I am always vulnerable. But this jungle is especially dangerous: there are many creatures here who would enjoy a meal of pig.'

'Ragallach, my friend,' Paedur said with a smile. 'You protect us during the day, you can depend on us to protect you at night.'

The Torc Allta started to nod, but then the were-change took him, dropping him to the ground, twisting and shaping his bones and muscles, turning him into a pig. He trotted up and sat in front of the fire, licking his forepaw with a long tongue.

Paedur pointed to the thorn circle with his hook. 'That will keep out all but the most inquisitive creatures. The fire should be enough to drive away the rest. Megan, how many darts have you?'

The Warrior Maid dug into her pouch and pulled out a dozen feathered thorns. 'I can shape some more,' she said quietly, 'but I'm not sure how accurate they would be. And I've no sleeping honey for them.'

'Make some darts anyway,' the bard said, 'their sting might be enough to deter some creatures.'

Something crashed through the undergrowth, bringing them all to their feet. Paedur and Faolan grabbed sticks and plunged them into the fire, while Megan brought her pipe to her lips. The creature, invisible in the darkness, moved around the circle of thorns before it clumped off into the night.

'Our smell attracts them,' Megan said. 'We smell of salt and fresh meat. And the odour of burning wood is curious to them.'

Ken crept closer to the fire and stared out into the darkness. 'I'm just wondering what else the smells will attract.'

Paedur lay down with his back to the fire. 'Ken and Megan will take first watch, Faolan and Ally the next. I'll take over before the dawn.'

'That is the most dangerous time,' Megan said glancing quickly at the bard. 'Those beasts which have not fed during the night will be desperate.'

The bard yawned. 'So long as we keep the fire burning, we should be fine.'

'The fires won't keep away humans,' the Warrior Maid added.

'There are no humans in the forest,' Paedur replied. Rolling over, he pulled his hood over his head, folded his arms across his chest and fell asleep.

He was wrong: from the trees and bushes, hundreds of dark human eyes watched the small group settle down for the night.

Scathach smelt smoke on the air.

The Grey Warrior stopped, breathing deeply, sorting through the dozens of odours — rich growth, thick mud, rotting vegetation, animal smells — until she had fixed the direction of the smoky smell. She knew then that they had stopped for the night. Whoever was leading them was clever, and obviously knew the dangers of moving through a pitch dark forest at night. Without being able to see the twisted roots, it was easy to catch and break an ankle, a low hanging branch could tear skin or even blind, and once there was a scent of blood on the air, then the beasts would swarm in to feed.

Scathach moved on. She knew she should have made herself a camp and waited until the dawn but her desire for vengeance drove her on. Her eyesight was a little better than most humans and when she had been training as a warrior, she had learned to fight and move in absolute darkness. Although she couldn't see clearly, she could make out the shapes of trees and bushes and her keen sense of smell warned her when an animal approached. However, most of the animals scented the bitter odour of her metal swords on the air, and avoided her.

Finally, Scathach stopped. There was a light in the distance, a twisting flickering spot of yellow-white light. Muttering a quick silent prayer to her gods, the Grey Warrior crept closer, moving completely silently now, testing each footstep before she pressed down on it. She was aware of animals in the undergrowth, also watching the small encampment, waiting for the fire to die down. Well, when she had finished with them, the beasts of the forest could have the remains.

The renegades had erected a screen of thorn bushes around the camp. Scathach tried to gauge the thickness of the thorns, wondering if it would be possible to push her way through. Two of the humans — the dark-haired girl and the red-haired boy — were sitting on either side of the fire, talking quietly together, but everyone else was asleep. The small pig was nestled close to the red-haired female. Scathach knew she would have to take the humans at night; if she waited for day-break, she would have to fight the were-beast as well. She had no doubts that she could defeat him, but why make her job any more difficult? The Grey Warrior looked up at the nearest tree. Its branches came over the edge of the screen of thorns. She smiled quickly. All she had to do was to climb the tree and drop down into the camp. It would take her a matter of heartbeats to dispatch them all.

Ken watched Megan shaping torns into darts with her knife, her small hands moving quickly, carving the wood into long needle-pointed slivers of wood. She saw him watching her and looked at him curiously. 'Do you find what I am doing so strange?' she asked.

Ken thought for a moment, then he nodded. 'I suppose I do. I've never seen anyone carve like you.'

'But do people not hunt in your time?'

'Not for food. Some hunt for sport.'

Megan returned to cutting the wood. 'Where I come from, you hunt for food. If you miss your shot, you will not get a second one, and so you will grow hungry. And in my lands, the hungry die, they have no defence against the bitter cold.'

'Do you miss your homeland?' Ken asked.

Megan considered for a moment before she finally shook her head. 'No. If I had stayed there, I would probably be married by now....' She saw his look of shock and stopped. 'What's wrong?'

'But, you're about Ally's age: fourteen. Surely you wouldn't marry so young.'

'In the Northlands, a man is old when he is thirty,' Megan said grimly. 'Women marry young.' She looked at Ken. 'How old will you be when you marry?'

Ken shrugged his shoulders. 'I don't know. I could be twenty or thirty I suppose. But I haven't even met anyone I like yet. I'm only thirteen,' he added.

Megan looked surprised. 'You choose your own bride?'

'Yes.'

The Warrior Maid nodded. 'I have heard of such things. Where I come from, marriages are arranged. I know my own mother did not meet my father until the morning of the wedding ceremony.'

'There are arranged marriages in my time also, but they are not so common.'

Megan returned to her carving. 'No, I am happy I left. I have seen a lot of the world, I have learned much.'

'Will you ever go back?'

'It would be difficult,' Megan admitted. 'After all we have experienced, it would seem so dull.'

Ken turned away, nodding. He knew exactly what she meant. This world — this dangerous, frightening world — seemed so real, while his own world, with its cars and computers, television and video, seemed false and imaginary. Here he felt so alive. He was turning back to ask Megan another question, when he saw the grim-faced woman drop down from the trees, two curved swords in her hands.

'Scathach!' he managed to scream, before she had launched herself forward, slashing at him with one sword, cutting at Megan with the other.

Ken threw himself backwards, stumbling into the fire in an explosion of sparks. He actually heard the sword blade hiss past his face.

Megan had instinctively raised her blow-pipe when the sword had come whistling out of the darkness. The blade had chopped through it, but the force of the blow had thrown her to one side.

Scathach spun. These creatures were blessed by the gods! They were still alive, and now she had lost the element of surprise. The others were rising to their feet, the bard taking up a position in front, left arm extended, the hook gleaming in the firelight. The warrior maid was standing behind and to his left, two short knives in her hands, while the golden-haired boy was to the right of the bard. The two red-haired humans were standing at the back, the girl beating at the boy's smouldering clothes. Scathach realised she would have to get past the bard first and get the Windlord before he worked his magic. She could then take care of the rest at her leisure.

Without a word, she launched her attack, her twin blades weaving a deadly pattern before her. Paedur caught the two blades on his hook, yellow-white sparks flying. The Grey Warrior struck again, and again he caught the blades, but the force of the combined blows drove him backwards. Scathach struck once more, putting all her weight behind the blow. Although Paedur caught the swords, the force of the blows spun him around. Another blow, which he caught on the edge of his hook, drove him to his knees. The fourth blow sent him sprawling, his arm numb.

Megan launched her two knives, but the Grey Warrior easily deflected them with her swords, sending them spinning off into the darkness.

Scathach saw the Windlord throw back his head and raise his hands. With a roar she dived towards him, her right sword pointed directly at his throat....

'Faolan!' Ally screamed as the woman bore down on him.

With a terrifying scream, a huge hairy beast dropped from the trees and snatched the sword from Scathach's hand. Another beast bore the Grey Warrior to the ground, pinning her down. Scathach struggled violently, but she was no match for the creature's enormous strength. More and more of the creatures dropped into the clearing, some of them carrying thick wooden clubs. The trees were filled with beasts who began screaming and whooping in what sounded like triumph.

All across the forest the night animals began to shout and roar their own calls until the sound was deafening. But as suddenly as it had begun, the calls stopped and the night returned to silence.

Eight of the creatures faced the humans. Two of them were holding Scathach, while another two wrapped her feet and arms with thick ropes of woven vines. It was difficult to make out their features in the flickering firelight, but they were long-haired, with flat, vaguely human faces and massive teeth-lined jaws.

'Gorillas,' Ken whispered. 'They look like gorillas.'

The dark-furred creatures sat down facing the humans, staring at them with small black eyes. Ragallach, still in his pig shape, trotted up to the nearest creature and nuzzled it with his blunt snout. The creature patted the pig's back with its thick- knuckled hand. Satisfied, Ragallach trotted back and lay down at Ally's feet.

'I think Ragallach is trying to tell us that they are friends,' Paedur murmured.

Faolan wrinkled his nose. 'There is the scent of magic about them,' he said quietly.

'Of course,' Paedur whispered, almost to himself. 'They must be the Gor Allta.'

Faolan glanced at him quickly. 'I thought they were legend.'

The bard shrugged. 'Obviously not.'

Ally leaned across Paedur's shoulder. 'What are they?'

'They are one of the were-folk clans, like Ragallach.'

'What do they turn into?' she asked in a whisper.

Paedur shook his head. 'I don't know.' He stood before the largest of the Gor Allta. Its eyes were bright and intelligent, but the bard was also aware of the huge jaw filled with jagged teeth. These animals were meat eaters. Keeping his expression neutral, knowing that many animals interpreted the human smile — bared teeth — as a threatening gesture, he bowed slowly. 'We thank you,' he said.

The Gor Allta looked at him unblinkingly, its broad hand scratching at its chest, and then it turned away, joining the other creatures huddled around the edges of the camp, close to the shadows. They had pulled Scathach into their midst. The Grey Warrior was trussed up with thick vines, but she had not cried out, nor wasted her energy in fighting the beasts' great strength, and the bard almost found himself admiring her courage. He turned back to his companions.

'What now?' Faolan asked.

'Now we wait,' Paedur said. He looked at Ken. 'Are you all right?'

The boy turned to show the scorch marks on his back. Portions of his hair had frizzled when he had rolled into the fire. 'I was lucky,' he smiled.

'You were,' the bard agreed. He glanced at Megan who was trying to fit together the two halves of her shattered blow-pipe. 'You were both lucky. But I'm beginning to think there was more than luck involved.' he added quietly.

'What do you mean?' Ken asked.

Paedur sank down in front of the fire, the orange flames washing over his face, turning his eyes to copper coins. Glancing over his shoulder to where the beasts crouched in the darkness, he lowered his voice. 'On the night before the Earthlord destroyed the Avenue of Standing Stones, the Gods of the De Danann Isle came to me.' He said it so casually that it took the others a few moments before they realised what he had said. Ally began to smile before she realised that the bard was serious.

'The Avenue of Standing Stones is — *was* — ancient and magical,' he continued. 'Apparently Ken unknowingly awoke the gods when he touched the prayer stones. They came just before dawn in shapes of mist and shadow. I spoke to the Lady Danu, Goddess of this island.' He paused and then added forcefully, looking at each of them in turn. 'This was no dream. The Lady Danu told me how Balor was abusing the Earthlord's power. Every time Colum uses his magic, he weakens the very fabric of this island. Deep in the core of this land, he has already churned up destructive energies. If we do not stop him, then there will come a point when he calls up his power and this whole island will be ripped apart.'

Megan raised her head. 'The shamans — the holy men — of my people say that the world will end in fire and destruction.'

Paedur nodded. 'I know that legend. Perhaps it is true.'

'But the world has not ended,' Ken said quickly. 'After all, we are from your future.'

'I know,' the bard murmured, 'but are there De Danann folk in your world? Is your world a place of magic? Do the Fomor and the Torc Allta, the nathair and the Gor Allta walk your world?'

Ken and Ally shook their heads.

'So you see,' Paedur continued with a faint smile. 'You might say that our world has ended.'

Faolan leaned forward across the fire, the flames colouring his golden hair a deep rich red. 'You said we had survived on this quest through more than luck ... what did you mean?' he asked.

'We have been helped by the gods - I'm convinced of it,' he added quickly, seeing the looks of disbelief on Ken, Ally's and Faolan's face. Only Megan nodded in agreement. She had no difficulty accepting the existence of the gods.

'The gods themselves cannot meddle directly in human affairs, but they often choose champions to act for them. I believe we are the chosen of the gods. If you can accept that, then everything that has happened so far begins to make more sense, from the moment when Ken and Ally were pulled back to this time. Now it doesn't really matter if you believe me or not,' he continued grimly. 'But what you should know is that tomorrow we will cross to the Fomor Isles ... and the gods of the De Danann Isle hold no sway there. The Fomor worship their own savage serpentine gods.' The bard smiled quickly. 'So whatever force — whether it is the help of the gods, or simple luck — that we have had with us so far, it will not cross to the serpent isle with us.'

'You're trying to tell us that things are going to get worse,' Ken smiled.

Paedur nodded. 'Precisely.'

The Forest of Caesir grew silent just before dawn, the night noises fading one by one. The Gor Allta who had been huddled together around the Grey Warrior, grew restless and began to move around the small encampment, their broad heads moving from side to side, their savage teeth exposed.

Faolan felt it first. Raising his head to the east, he said simply, 'Sunrise.'

And the Gor Allta changed.

The were-change knocked them to the ground, shuddering through their bodies. In the flickering shadows it was difficult to make out what was happening, but the creatures seemed to be shrinking, drawing in on themselves, the thick hair that covered their bodies thinning out. There were sounds of snapping and tearing as bones and muscles rearranged themselves, and the creatures' harsh grunting cries turned softer, gentler.

Ragallach, who had also changed with the sunrise, rose to his feet and stretched his arms high, muscles popping. 'You were lucky our friends arrived last night,' he grunted.

'There was no luck involved, brother-beast, we had been following you since you entered our domain.' The voice was surprisingly soft, almost child-like, and completely out of character with the short, bulky, hairy man that rose from the ground. All around him, the Gor Allta, now transformed into a human shape were coming to their feet.

Ragallach stepped forward and stretched out his hand. The short hairy man clasped his forearm. 'Brother-beast,' the Torc Allta said quietly. 'We thank you for helping us.'

The short man nodded quickly. 'Our little brothers, the Simpeansai, warned us that the Fomor and their serpent beasts had flown deep into our lands, pursuing soft-skins.' The Gor Allta smiled, and while his face had changed from that of a beast into something human, he retained his savage animal teeth. His smiled was terrifying. 'I mean no disrespect when I call you that,' he added.

Paedur stepped up beside Ragallach. 'We know that. I would give you our names, but since you have not given me yours, I presume you prefer it that way.'

The man bowed slightly. 'We are the Gor Allta, the Beast Folk. We believe that there is a magic in names. Perhaps it would be better if we did not share names just yet.'

'I understand.'

The beast-man spread his arms wide. 'This is our land. We will take you where you want to go in safety.'

'Why?' Megan asked suspiciously. 'You know little about us. Why should you help us.'

The Gor Allta stared at the Warrior Maid with his black eyes for a moment, then he said, 'You are a hunter, and you are right to be suspicious. It will keep you alive so much longer. We will help you because the Fomor were pursuing you. The Fomor's enemies are our friends.' He gestured towards Ragallach. 'And because a brother-beast travels with you, not as a servant or a slave, but as an equal companion.'

Megan nodded quickly, accepting the answer.

'What will you do with Scathach?' Paedur asked.

The Gor Allta turned his stocky head to look at the woman. 'I have not decided yet,' he said quietly. 'She fights with the serpent-folk?' he asked.

The bard nodded. 'She is close to Balor.'

The beast-man smiled again. 'Since the beginning of time the Fomor and the Gor Allta have made war upon one another. Sometimes the gods favour us and we triumph, but lately the Fomor have been winning more and more battles. Recently they have even started sending troops into the Forest. In a recent skirmish, they captured our leader. Even now he is being held on the Fomor Isle.' He looked at the woman again. 'If this woman is important to the Emperor, perhaps they might be willing to swap prisoners.'

Paedur smiled. 'I think they would do that.'

'Now, soft-skins, where do you wish to go in the Forest of Caesir?'

'We too need to rescue someone held prisoner on the Fomor Isles. Will you lead us to the coast?'

The beast-man nodded. 'If you go to the isle, you will not return.'

'We have no choice,' Paedur said simply.

The Gor Allta shrugged, turning away. 'It is your decision. But the Fomor will eat you,' he added.

Balor crouched on the floor of the map room, sitting in the middle of the model of the De Danann Isles. He liked to come here and look on the detailed map, to stretch his arms wide and touch the continent from side to side, and think that all this was his to control.

But the Emperor didn't have that feeling now. His single human eye traced a path from Falias south to the Forest of Caesir. He had had the humans in his control, but once again they had escaped, and not only had they stolen his own nathair, they had left a gaping hole in the centre of the capital as a reminder of their escape. Twenty of his elite Fomor had flown south with Scathach in pursuit of the renegades. Fourteen had returned, and even the Grey Warrior was missing.

It was as if the gods themselves were working against him.

And yet he prayed to Quataz, the Feathered Serpent, the God of the Fomor. The De Danann gods the human-kind worshipped were weak; surely they couldn't stand against his own magic and the power of his serpent god?

Balor looked at the map again. Why had the humans flown south? Why not west or east or back into the Northlands, where the Fomor would not be able to follow? There was rebellion in the far west, and the city of Murias had declared itself independent. The renegades would have found safety there.

Why south?

Balor came to his feet. He was still stiff and bruised from his fall into the pit and there was a deep dent in his metal mask.

The Gor Allta inhabited the Forest of Caesir. Beasts by night, beast-men by day, they were incredibly strong and the natural enemy of the Fomor. Were the humans attempting to rally the Gor Allta to fight with the human-kind in an attempt to overthrow him and his Fomor troops?

The Emperor nodded. It was possible, very possible.

'Cichal,' he shouted.

The door opened immediately and the Fomor Officer stepped into the room. Like the Emperor he was bruised from his fall and a jagged cut on his tail was coated in a thick covering of healing green mud.

'The renegades are in the Forest of Caesir,' Balor said, pointing to the spot on the map. 'I fear they may be attempting to bring the Gor Allta around to their cause....'

Cichal nodded. 'There has been some trouble there recently. But we captured one of their leaders.'

'I want you to take as many of your Troop as you can spare from their duties here in the city and fly south to your home island. I will give you a message for Morc, the King of the Isles, instructing him to give you as many officers as he can. You should be able to raise an army of ten thousand Fomor.'

'What then, lord?'

Balor's smile turned savage. 'Then take your Troops into the forest and destroy the Gor Allta. Destroy the forest too if you have to!' The Emperor's laughter echoed around the chamber. 'These renegade humans think they are clever, but they will learn that they cannot stand against the might of Balor.'

The sticky and smelly forest air changed to the fresher, cleaner salt smell of the sea. The Forest of Caesir ended suddenly, the last trees coming right up to the water's edge. The Gor Allta leaned forward and held aside the dangling branches.

'The Fomor Isles,' he said simply.

After the dark, muted greens and browns of the forest, the sea looked brilliantly blue. No waves washed against the shore and its flat and mirror-calm surface was shot through with swirling patches of red. The largest Fomor island was directly in front of them, while the second, slightly smaller island was off to the right. The six smaller islands which were part of the archipelago were hidden by the headland.

The Gor Allta pointed to the red stain in the water. 'We will give you a boat to get you across to the island, but you must take care to avoid the red oil. It is a living organism from the sea bed and it feeds off solid matter, the wood of your boat, for example, or your own flesh. If you fall into the water, you will die quickly.'

'Is there no other way to the island?' Paedur asked.

'There is a bridge,' the beast-man said. 'It is made in three sections, but the third part which connects the bridge to the mainland is usually drawn up until it is needed. Naturally, the bridge is heavily guarded by Fomor.' He pointed with a stubby-fingered hand. 'There are towers on the island — you can just about see them peeking through the tops of the trees. They are guarded day and night.'

The bard stared at the wooden towers, his sharp eyesight picking out the figure of a Fomor guard moving to and fro. Without turning around, he asked, 'When will you attempt to trade Scathach for your captured leader?'

'Today. Before the night and the were-change takes us.'

'Where is the bridge?'

The beast-man pointed to the left. 'Just around the headland.'

'Make as much noise as you can,' Paedur said. 'We will slip in while they are distracted.'

'The beasts will be able to scent you,' the Gor Allta reminded him.

'If we find the Earthlord's family, we'll be able to use my windmagic to flee,' Faolan said. 'Once Colum sees that his family is safe, he can use his power to destroy Balor.'

Paedur shook his head. 'Let's not plan that far ahead just yet. If we manage to escape from the islands with our lives, I'll be satisfied.'

'You could walk away, human-kind,' the beast-man said.

Paedur turned to look at the others before he answered, speaking for all of them. 'No. It's far too late to walk away.'

'It begins,' Ragallach said, raising his huge head to the late afternoon sky. Moments later, the sounds of the Gor Allta's howling echoed across the forest, sending birds screaming into the sky, setting the Simpean-sai screaming in their trees.

'Let's go,' Paedur said. He was sitting in the prow of the narrow wooden canoe the Gor Allta had made for them, hacking out the centre of a tree trunk with stones and slivers of fire- hardened wood. Ken had been dubious when he had learned that they were going to make a boat in a single afternoon, but four Gor Allta had worked steadily with their primitive tools and had shaped the canoe and four paddles long before the afternoon light had begun to fade.

'I didn't think they'd do it in time,' the red-haired boy said to Paedur. 'They were only using stones....'

'It is not the tools,' Paedur said with a smile, 'but the skill. Neither you nor I could have shaped that boat with blades of iron.'

They watched the Gor Allta slide the canoe into the water and then rock it from side to side, allowing water to splash in over the sides. When they were satisfied that there were no cracks or splits in the wood that would allow water to seep in, they pulled the canoe out of the water, dried it out with moss and then rubbed it inside and out with the juice of dark purple berries. Then, their task complete, the four Gor Allta simply walked away without a backward glance.

The leader of the Gor Allta appeared out of the forest. He was wearing a breastplate of polished wood and carried an enormous oval shield and two stone-tipped spears. 'We have done what we can for you, soft-skins. The boat is safe, and will not sink beneath you. Avoid the red stain on the water. The brothers have coated your craft with a juice which the stain dislikes, but the water will gradually wash it away.' The Gor Allta turned away, but paused before he vanished into the forest. 'If your task is successful, remember us, the Gor Allta. Once we were a proud race; now we live like savages in this forest.'

Paedur nodded. 'If our mission is successful, and we defeat Balor, then all the De Danann Isle will know the part the Gor Allta played in his downfall. I swear it as a bard.'

The beast man nodded once more and vanished into the forest, the trees closing in and claiming him.

'What now?' Faolan asked.

Paedur nodded across the dark water. 'The Fomor Isle. Everyone into the boat.'

The noise was incredible.

Poc ground his teeth in frustration, forked tongue flickering madly. His watch tower faced the forest and so he couldn't see what was happening on the other side of the island, but it sounded as if the Gor Allta and the entire forest had risen up and attacked the bridge.

The Fomor hated this guard duty. It was usually given as a punishment, but he hadn't actually done anything ... well, perhaps he had eaten too many of the fat wine grapes, and perhaps he had fallen asleep, but what harm had been done? He had been guarding the grape harvest and what creature in their right mind was going to attack a cartload of grapes? So he had been placed on this guard duty, watching the dark forest across the water. What a waste of time. The Gor Allta couldn't swim and even if they could the red stain in the water would feed off them. The beast-men couldn't fly nathair — so where was the danger?

Poc looked across the tree tops towards the source of the sound, wishing he could be where the action was.

'Quickly now, quickly,' Paedur urged his companions. With swift movements, Faolan and Ken, who were sitting side by side and Ally and Megan who were sitting behind them, dipped their oars into the water and the canoe leapt forward. Ragallach sat in the back of the canoe, using another paddle to steer the craft in towards the isle.

'Again,' Paedur hissed. He was in the prow of the boat, staring hard at the guard in the top of the tower. The Fomor was looking away towards the source of the noise, but all he had to do was turn and he would see the long dark shape of the canoe on the still water. 'Again.' The oars dipped and dipped again.

Suddenly Megan hissed in alarm. The end of her oar was covered in an oily red liquid. As she watched, the liquid burned through the wood and then began to creep up the handle of the paddle. The warrior maid quickly dropped the paddle into the water and picked up one of the spares the Gor Allta had cut for them.

'We must have come through some of the red stain,' Paedur said. 'Let's hope it doesn't find our craft too tasty. We must hurry.'

Another dozen strokes brought them very close to the shore, and they had now passed below the level of the watch tower. The bard allowed himself a smile of satisfaction ... and then he felt dampness under his knee. When he looked down he discovered that a tiny trickle of water was seeping into the boat. He turned around and saw Ragallach lift his paw. Without a word the beast showed it to the bard: his paw was wet. They both knew what had happened; the red stain was eating away at the wooden boat. It was now a race to see if they could reach the shore before they sank.

'Faster,' Paedur urged. 'Faster.'

But the rowers were tiring now, especially Ken and Ally who were unused to this hard physical exercise.

'Another four strokes,' Paedur said.

The paddles dipped, but not all at the same time and the canoe didn't go very far.

'We've sprung a leak!' Ken said loudly, immediately lowering his voice.

'I know,' Paedur said calmly. 'That's why we must row. Now, on my command — row!'

The paddles dipped neatly into the water, pushing the boat forward.

'Row!'

Again, the paddles dipped and the canoe surged forward in the water.

Pink-tinged water was seeping in from a dozen places now. A long crack appeared directly beneath Ally and the red-stained water flowed through.

'Once more,' Paedur urged.

With a final surge of strength, the rowers sent the canoe forward ... and then it shuddered onto the beach.

'Out, out,' Paedur hissed desperately, hopping out of the boat and attempting to drag it up out of the water. Ragallach hopped out at the other end and pushed the boat up onto the shingle beach. Ally almost fell over the side as she attempted to scramble away from the stained water, but the Torc Allta caught her and helped her out of the boat.

'Get out of the water,' Paedur whispered. 'Quickly Ragallach,' he commanded, pointing over the beast's shoulder. The Torc Allta turned — and spotted a large patch of red stain flowing in towards the boat. He splashed up onto the beach leaving the boat rocking gently in the shallows.

They watched in silence as the red stain flowed in around the boat, bubbling up from beneath, seeping in through the tiny cracks, widening them, eating through the dark wood. The liquid stain turned sticky and tacky when it hit the air. It bubbled up around the wood, coating the canoe in a pink jelly-like substance.

The boat lurched, settling deeper into the water as the bottom of the canoe was completely devoured. There was a crack and the boat split in two. The water was a bright blood red as more of the stain, drawn by the scents of wood, swarmed in. The boat was now invisible, completely covered in the sticky red mass. Huge bubbles rose and burst with faint pops, reeking with a foul-smelling gas.

Gradually the red stain sank back into the water, the bubbles grew fewer and the water gradually turned from a deep red to a pink and then finally to a pale blue. All trace of the boat had vanished.

The six companions watched in silence. When they turned away from the beach, they found they were facing a Fomor warrior.

Poc raised his stone sword. 'I came down here because I saw the waters had turned red, and I wondered what the stain was feeding off,' he hissed. 'Now, should I bring you before the king, or toss you back into the water?'

Poc slipped his hand into a long narrow pouch he wore on his belt, and pulled out what looked like a small pale-skinned worm. It shuddered awake, rising up in the palm of his claw and regarded the humans suspiciously with its slit-pupilled yellow eyes. It hissed at them, its narrow forked tongue surprisingly long.

The Fomor ran the back of a long nail over the creature's leathery skin. 'Let us wait here while the peist brings the news back to the fort.' He tossed the worm into the air. Two almost transparent wings flapped open and held the peist in mid-air for a moment before it spun around and set off inland. They all looked up, following the creature's path through the forest, its wings shimmering in a rainbow of colours.

Poc's momentary inattention gave Megan the chance she was waiting for. Stepping behind Ragallach's bulky body, she slipped the broken blowpipe from her pouch and quickly spat a dart at the Fomor. She was aiming for his throat, but the beast raised a claw and the dart struck him in the tip of a long-nailed claw. While he looked at it, wondering where the feathered sliver of wood had come from, another dart struck him in the jaw. This time he saw the black-haired female fire at him. With a hiss of rage, the Fomor lurched forward, his great stone sword held in both hands ... and crashed to the ground, the tip of his sword plunging deep in the earth.

'We don't have much time,' Paedur said quickly. 'This whole area will be swarming with Fomor as soon as the peist reaches the main caves. We need to get inside the Fomor caves, into the cells. But I don't know how,' he added.

'Why don't we allow ourselves to be captured,' Ken said simply. He was kneeling beside the sleeping Fomor, the creature's long-bladed stone knife in his hands. Pulling up his trouser leg, he tied the knife to the side of his calf with three lengths of vine. Fixing his trousers, he stood up and moved his leg. The knife shifted, but didn't fall out.

'Don't be so ridiculous,' Ally snapped. 'We haven't come all this way simply to be captured.'

But Paedur nodded quickly. 'No, I think it's a brilliant plan. The Fomor don't know how many of us are here. If they were to capture two or three of us, that might satisfy them and they would then call off the search. It would also allow those who remained free to help those on the inside.'

'You're forgetting one thing,' Ally reminded him. 'What's to stop the Fomor simply killing us the moment they capture us?'

'Because we're too valuable to them. Before they do anything to us, they will want to check with the Emperor. That will give us the time we need.'

'We're wasting time,' Ken reminded him. 'I'm willing to be taken prisoner. Now, who will come with me?'

Ragallach started to speak, but his words ended in a grunt as the were-change took him, twisting his body, bending it back into its animal shape. Although the sun had not yet sunk below the horizon, the Torc Allta's body was still in tune with the cooler northern climate, where the sun sank earlier in the day. Raising his small head high, his flat snout wrinkled and then, with a squeak, he vanished into the dense undergrowth.

'They're coming,' Paedur whispered. 'Faolan, come with me. Megan and Ally — will you go with Ken?' Without waiting for a reply, he added, 'Don't worry, we'll come for you.' He grabbed Faolan's arm and the two disappeared into the bushes — just as the twilight sky overhead darkened as four nathair appeared. Three were black, but one was an enormous grey. Then the bushes all around them parted as a Troop of Fomor appeared, weapons levelled.

The grey nathair landed in the midst of the clearing and the Fomor Officer slid down. As he turned to face them, they saw that he wore a metallic eye patch over his left eye.

'Cichal,' Ally breathed in terror.

The huge beast approached, his massive head turning from side to side, forked tongue flickering, attempting to sort through the odours. But the red stain had tainted the air with its own rich salty tang. Cichal stopped before the humans and folded his arms across his chest. He stared at them unblinkingly with his single yellow eye.

'You certainly look human,' he said in his hissing accent. 'You smell human.'

'We are human,' Megan said simply.

The beast nodded. 'For a while there I thought you were demons, or gods sent to this world. You have caused me much trouble, human-kind. You have made me lose face in front of the Emperor, you have made my hatchling lose face before me and the Emperor. My hatchling is now missing. You very nearly made me lose my life. I have fought with some of the most dangerous creatures on the De Danann Isles. I have done battle with men, beasts and were-creatures. But none of them ever caused me as much trouble as your band of renegades.' He sighed with a great hiss. 'I suppose the bard, the Windlord and the Torc Allta are still in the forest stirring up the Gor Allta.'

Managing to mask her surprise, Megan shrugged. 'I'm not sure where they are,' she said truthfully.

Cichal turned to look at the Forest of Caesir across the water. Spots of light could be seen moving through the trees. 'No matter. We know you are attempting to raise a Gor Allta army to attack this isle or maybe even Falias. But you have wasted your time. I have practically every Fomor in Falias and the surrounding countryside under my command. At first light, we will carry the fight into the forest and attack the beast-men. I have orders to burn the forest to the ground if I have to.'

'Why at first light?' Ken wondered.

'Because even the mighty Fomor would be no match for the Gor Allta in their beast shape at night,' Megan said.

Cichal nodded. 'Exactly.' He turned away. 'Bring them,' he said to his Troop. 'I'm sure the king will wish to see them ... before we eat them!'

Morc had ruled the Fomor Isles for as long as anyone could remember. He was rumoured to be the oldest Fomor in existence ... indeed, there were some rumours that he was actually the first of the serpent Fomor that the gods created. Once, he had built an empire that had stretched beyond the borders of the De Danann Isle, and he had made the Fomor creatures to be feared even into the continent of the Black Folk and across to the west to the country of the Copper Skins.

But he had grown old. Old and tired. He had conquered the world, gone further and seen more than any living creature, and suddenly he had discovered that there was nothing else to do. He couldn't even die because in his youth he had saved an ancient human wizard from the terrible wingless dragons that roamed the earth then, but which had since vanished. The wizard had granted him a single wish, and Morc had said that he wanted to live forever.

And the wizard had granted him his desire.

So now he was ageless. He could still be killed of course, but he didn't age. Time had stopped for him on a summer's day, a thousand years previously. The wizard had tried to warn him, had begged him to choose another wish, but Morc hadn't been prepared to listen. He understood now why the wizard had asked him to choose something else. Morc had seen his world change and change and change again. He had seen his wives and children grow old and die, leaving him alone. He had watched the empire he had created fade away, returning the proud Fomor race to little more than warring savages. Once they had known the secret of working metal; now they knew only stone. Once, all the known world trembled at the name of Morc the Pitiless; now he was virtually unknown outside the small archipelago of the Fomor Isles. He grew grapes, and had spent the last twenty summers writing down the history of the world as he remembered it, carefully chipping the angular Fomor script onto tablets of stone. It amused him to think that some day someone might find and read them, and wonder about the name of Morc the Fomor.

And everything had been fine; the ancient king had even managed to find peace of a sort until Balor had come along.

Morc knew that people thought he was Balor's father, but the king knew he could not count the Emperor amongst his many children. The boy's father had been one of Morc's most trusted officers. He had vanished along with the boy's mother, a coal-black witch, on an expedition to the Dark Continent in search of an enormous jewelled idol.

Even as a child, Balor had been dangerous and almost from the day he was born he had been forced to wear a leather half-mask to cover his face. When he had turned thirteen summers the boy had discovered his deadly talent for turning people to stone by removing the mask, and Morc had very nearly ordered the boy set adrift in a boat on more than one occasion. There were times — like now — when he bitterly regretted not doing that. Now Balor ruled the De Danann Isle, and he had once again made the Fomor into creatures to be feared and hated.

And now Balor wanted to destroy the Forest of Caesir, and all the Gor Allta because he suspected that a group of renegade humans were inciting a rebellion.

Deep in thought, the ancient king swept through the long tunnels, the guards coming to attention. Three of the humans had been captured by one of the border guards. Although they had somehow managed to overpower him, the officer had set free his peist and within moments the area had been flooded with troops. By a very good chance, Cichal himself had been amongst those to capture the humans.

A pair of massive doors loomed up. The plain wooden panels were embossed with Fomor masks, perfect images of the king which had been carved a thousand years ago, by an artist whose bones had long since crumbled into dust.

The enormous Presence Chamber had been carved out of the living rock. Over the centuries the room had been enlarged and although it had originally been windowless, small circular windows had been added over the years, which now threw shafts of light into the centre of the room, though the corners still remained in shadow. Tattered remnants of war banners hung on the walls. The only piece of furniture in the room was a throne shaped from the bones of the long extinct wingless nathair. A single shaft of light illuminated the throne.

The room was crowded with Fomor warriors, all of them heavily armed and armoured. They parted before Morc, bowing their heads and slapping their breastplates as a mark of respect. Although the king was ancient, he was still taller and broader than the average Fomor, and his features were cruder, more brutish than those of the present generation. His snout was blunter, and he walked with a definite hunch, with his head thrust forward. His tail was longer also, and it trailed behind him, like a living peist.

Morc expected to find himself facing a dangerous band of

prisoners. Instead, he found himself facing a red-haired boy and girl and a warrior maid from the Ice Fields of Thusal.

The king looked at Cichal, his forked tongue flickering wildly. 'This is it! You dragged me from my vineyards for this?' he demanded.

'They are dangerous, my lord. The Emperor himself has ordered....'

'The Emperor does not give orders on these islands,' Morc snapped. He slumped into his bone chair and glared at the humans. 'They are whelps, not yet into adulthood,' he remarked.

Cichal nodded.

'And dangerous you say?' Morc continued.

'Most definitely, my lord.'

'They do not look dangerous.'

'That is their cunning, my lord. For who would suspect whelps of planning a rebellion.'

The king nodded, suddenly uninterested. If Balor couldn't control a few human whelps, then there was little hope for him. He looked at the children again, his chin resting in his claw. What was he going to do with them? No doubt Balor wanted them sent back, but Morc had been a king long before the Emperor's grandparents had been born ... and the king of the Fomor Isles wasn't going to take orders from anyone. No; he would deal with the human-kind here. Morc straightened slowly, what passed for a smile drawing his gums back from his ragged teeth. He hadn't eaten human flesh for a long, long time. He could feel his stomach rumble at the thought of a fresh human child.

'What does Balor want me to do with these?' he asked Cichal.

'He wants them returned to Falias under the tightest security.'

Morc nodded. 'As I thought. But I am afraid I will not be sending them back to the Emperor. They came to the Fomor Isles of their own accord, even though they must have known that these islands are sacred to the Fomor. They have broken our laws; their very presence here offends us. They must be punished....'

'But the Emperor...' Cichal began.

'I rule the Fomor Isles,' Morc thundered. 'And though he may be Emperor of the human-kind, Balor is still one of my subjects; he is answerable to me. Take them away,' he shouted, coming to his feet. 'Prepare a feast. Tonight we will feast on human whelp!'

Ken thought he was going to throw up. The Fomor king was going to eat them. 'Tonight we will feast on human whelp!' he had said. The words kept going round and around in his head. Now he knew why he had always detested serpents.

It had taken a few moments for his words to sink in, and by the time Ken fully understood what he had said — that they would be cooked and eaten at a feast — six Fomor had appeared, caught them by the arms and dragged them from the Presence Chamber. He barely noticed the warren of tunnels they were marched through, but both Ally and Megan took careful note of their route, realising that they might need this information if they ever escaped.

Some of the caverns were enormous, and seemed to have been created by linking several caves together, while others were barely wide enough to allow the two Fomor and their human captive to pass through side by side. Everything was touched with a sickly yellow light that seemed to flow from the walls themselves, and it was only as she got close to a wall that Ally realised it was covered in what looked like a white fungus. It was the fungus that was glowing softly. Some of the walls had been cut with crude pictures and sharp notches that vaguely resembled the ogham writing she had seen on old Irish monuments.

At first the tunnels were densely populated, and for the first time Ally saw female and young Fomor. The females were smaller than the males and their features were finer, more delicate — almost more human, she decided — and their scales shimmered with a dozen vibrant colours, almost as if they had been oiled. Curiously, the young Fomor were very serpent-like. They were skinny, without the heavier armour plating of their parents, and their flesh looked soft and green. Their tails curled up over the back of their heads and they hadn't developed the heavy talons of adulthood.

The guards led them away from the densely populated tunnels, and down into narrow, damp and foul-smelling caverns that were obviously older. These were gloomier, the wall fungus no longer shining as brightly, and in places whole patches had faded, plunging that portion of the tunnel into darkness. The floors and ceiling of the upper tunnels were smooth and clear, but here stalactites clung to the ceiling, while stalagmites jutted up from the floor. Some of these had ancient-looking symbols and crude pictures carved into them. Most of the stalactites were moist with clear liquid, and were obviously still growing, though Ally knew that the biggest ones had taken many centuries to reach their present size. At one point they crossed an enormous cavern filled with Fomor bones. Some were white and bright but many, especially those close to the bottom of the pile, were ancient and yellow, and altogether more beast-like. They reminded Ally of crocodile skulls. Beyond this chamber the tunnel narrowed dramatically, until it was barely high enough for a single Fomor to walk through. Here, Ally could see the long picture panels that had been cut into the stone in the ancient past. They were painted in simple reds and black, and seemed to tell the history of a Fomor warrior who battled a host of half-humans, beast-folk and other, less easily identifiable creatures.

The tunnel ended in a broad platform. Beyond the platform, the ground simply vanished into a sheer drop at the bottom of which was a thin red-white line. Ken inched forward and peered out over the edge of the platform — and immediately wished he hadn't. The blast of heat that washed over his face made him realise that he was looking down onto a river of volcanic rock.

'If you fall it will take you a long time to reach the bottom,' one of the Fomor guards hissed.

The tunnel continued on the far side of the chasm. A sturdy looking rope bridge stretched from side to side. As the first Fomor stepped onto it, it creaked and swayed alarmingly.

'Is it safe?' Ally whispered.

The officer stepped back. 'It is designed to hold the weight of one Fomor at a time,' he said, with a note of pride in his voice. 'Any more than that and it will snap beneath the weight. So one Fomor can hold the bridge against an army. And of course, the bridge can always be cut,' he added. He pushed Ally forward. 'Now you. Go.'

It took an enormous effort of will to make her way across the swaying bridge. She could see through the wooden slats beneath her feet, and the heat and smell coming up from the volcanic stream below made her eyes water and her nose run. Clutching both sides of the bridge, she forced her feet to move, absolutely terrified that the next step would take her through the wood. As she neared the centre of the bridge, the swaying motion became more noticeable. It began to rock from side to side. A tiny sliver of wood cracked away beneath her feet and slowly spiralled into the inferno far below. Ally fell to her knees, clutching the sides so tightly the rope burned into her hands, her eyes squeezed shut. Her legs felt like jelly.

'Move,' the Fomor shouted. Sick with fear, Ally barely heard him.

One of the guards squeezed Ken's shoulder. 'She is from your brood?' he demanded.

Ken looked from him to Megan. 'He's asking are you related,' the dark-haired girl said.

'She is my sister.'

The Fomor grunted, not fully understanding the word. He had been hatched from a clutch of a dozen eggs; the brood were the closest he had to a brother or sister. 'Bring her to the other side.' He shoved Ken forward onto the wooden bridge.

Two things terrified Ken. Snakes were one; he really hated snakes, cold, slimy horrible things with dead eyes. And heights. He couldn't stand heights. When he was four, his father had taken Ally and himself up in a hot air balloon. They had both been petrified, imagining that they were going to fall or that the basket was going to break. Since then neither of them could stand heights. Fixing his eyes on his crouching sister, Ken forced himself to move across the wooden planks. His fingers and toes were tingling madly and his stomach was churning. He had to keep swallowing, and although waves of heat were coming up from below, he could actually feel ice-cold sweat trickle down along his spine.

'Move, whelp!' a Fomor roared.

'The height of the bridge and the swaying motion frightens them,' Megan said.

The Fomor looked at her unbelievingly.

'Is there nothing you fear, Fomor?' she asked.

'Nothing,' he said proudly.

'Heights hold no fear for me,' Megan added. 'Let me go to them.'

The Fomor looked at Ken, who had now slowed down to a stop, his feet barely inching forward, moving as if his eyes were closed.

'If you leave them much longer out there,' Megan added, 'you will find that their flesh will not be good to eat. Surely you know that fear releases fluids into the flesh which sours its taste?'

The six Fomor looked at one another. They knew what the girl was talking about. The flesh of a beast which had been frightened before it was slain was tougher, sharper than a beast that had remained calm until the end.

'You have no fear of heights?' the Fomor asked.

'No,' Megan said firmly. 'Like you, I am a warrior.'

The beast nodded. 'Bring them across.'

Megan moved quickly out onto the swaying bridge. Ken felt the sudden motion and froze, abruptly feeling as if all the air had been punched out of his lungs. He shouted with fright when he felt the hand on his shoulder.

'It's me, Ken. It's me,' Megan said soothingly. 'I want you to walk forward to Ally. Don't look down. Just stare straight ahead and imagine you're standing on a flat, paved road. I'll be right behind you. I'll hold you,' she added. She could feel Ken trembling, could feel the faint vibration of his thundering heart through his skin, and realised that he was truly terrified. She continued talking to him, her voice soothing, calming.

Ken walked slowly forward. The muscles in his legs were taut with tension and his thighs were aching.

They stopped beside Ally. She was still crouched down on the bridge, eyes locked shut. Megan knelt down, pulling Ken down beside her. 'This is our chance,' she hissed. 'The beasts cannot follow us — at least not while we're on the bridge. Have you still got the knife?' she asked Ken.

He blinked at her until her words sank in, then he touched the side of his leg where he had hidden the knife taken from the Fomor on the beach. 'I have it.'

'Take it out now. I'll shield you from the beasts.'

'Hurry up,' one of the Fomor shouted. 'Walk to the far side.'

Ken slid the knife free. The blade and handle had been shaped from a single piece of stone, then polished to a mirror shine. Leather straps had been wrapped around the handle.

'Once we reach the far side, cut the bridge,' Megan commanded.

Ken nodded quickly. Now that he had something to concentrate on, he felt his head clearing.

Megan helped Ally to her feet, talking quietly and calmly to her, encouraging her as she had encouraged Ken, moving her slowly towards the far side of the bridge. 'Nearly there, Ally. Nearly there. Another step, just one more.'

As soon as they had reached the far side, the Fomor Officer called, 'Stay there. Stay where you are.' One of the beasts immediately set out across the bridge, his great weight setting it swaying madly from side to side.

'Now, Ken. Now!' Megan shouted.

Gripping the blade in both hands, Ken slashed it down against the thick ropes that anchored the bridge in place. The stone blade bounced off the rope.

With a hiss of rage, the Fomor dragged his sword free and began to move as quickly as possible across the bridge.

Ken dragged the edge of the blade back and forth against the rope. A single strand gave way.

Hissing shouts of rage came from the other side of the bridge as the rest of the Fomor realised what Ken was doing. The Fomor on the bridge paused, undecided, wondering whether to continue towards the human-kind or to make his way back.

Another strand parted, quickly followed by four more, and the bridge lurched to one side.

The officer hissed in alarm, turned and raced back.

One of the supporting ropes snapped and the bridge sagged, all its weight shifting to one side. The Fomor dropped his sword and threw himself forward just as the the heavy ropes parted with loud snapping reports. He crashed onto the ledge and his fellow officers hauled him to safety. The bridge hung down against one side of the chasm for a few moments before its own weight pulled it from the stones, and it fell in a great twisting coil into the river of molten rock far below. An explosion of yellow-white flame erupted as it struck.

The Fomor officer raised a claw and shook it at the three humans. 'Do not think you have escaped us human-kind. You are trapped. You have destroyed the only exit from the Fomor dungeons. You have condemned yourselves and the other prisoners to death!'

Paedur and Faolan finally stopped running when they reached a tiny
pool, far from the coast. The Windlord collapsed onto the ground
and dipped his hand into the chill water, but Paedur caught his hand,
shaking his head silently. Ragallach, in his pig shape, broke through
the brush after them and trotted up to the water's edge. His moist
snout wrinkled and then he bent his head to drink.

'It's safe,' Paedur murmured, scooping up some of the chill water
in his hand. Faolan drank deeply, splashing water onto his face and
neck, before finally wiping his hands on the front of his jerkin.

'We shouldn't stay here,' Paedur advised.

'Why not?' Faolan asked.

Paedur pointed to the soft mud around the pool. In the dim light,
Faolan could just about make out the hundreds of pointed bird tracks
around it. Some of the claw marks were bigger than his own feet,
and the Windlord decided he didn't want to meet the bird that had
made those tracks.

'What now?' Faolan asked.

The bard pointed to the left with his hook, in towards the centre
of the island, which was dominated by a tree covered mountain. 'We
don't have very much time. The Fomor will discover soon enough
that we're not with the Gor Allta. If they really set out to find us,
then there's no way we'll be able to hide. They'll smell us out.' He
pulled his cloak tighter around his shoulder. 'We'll go this way.'

'Why?' Faolan asked, tiredly.

Paedur lifted his hook. The lines of script cut into the metal were
sparkling slightly in the gloom. 'Because there is old magic in the
air. Let's see where it's coming from.'

Ragallach suddenly stopped. The pig turned and rose up on his
hind legs, squealing quietly.

Faolan and Paedur turned and faced they way they had come.
But the jungle was dark and quiet.

Faolan threw back his head, feeling the night breeze flow across his skin. Taking a deep breath, he relaxed, closing his eyes, allowing the wind odours to carry their message.

'Fomor, nathair and the Gor Allta.' His voice was little more than a whisper. 'Fire and blood. The Fomor are attacking the Gor Allta!' His eyes snapped open.

Paedur grabbed his arm. 'We've even less time than I thought. Let's go. If the Fomor rescue Scathach, they'll know we're not with the Gor Allta. We have to get into the dungeons!'

As they pushed their way through the undergrowth, Faolan turned to look towards the mainland, where the wind had carried its message of destruction. He wondered what was happening there.

The Gor Allta beast-men marched right up to the bridge that led to the Fomor Isle and offered to trade the Emperor's Grey Warrior for their own captured leader. Morc himself had come down to meet the Gor Allta. With Cichal by his side, he strode across the bridge connecting the island to the mainland, and faced the beast-men across the missing centre section of the bridge. Directly below the break in the bridge the water was red with the living stain, kept there by the refuse the Fomor threw into the water. It also ensured that none of the Gor Allta would attempt to swim across.

A hundred shaggy-haired beast-men faced the two Fomor. One stepped forward and walked to the very edge of the bridge. He put his hands on his hips and bared his huge yellow teeth. 'We want to make a deal with you, Fomor,' he grunted.

Morc drew himself up to his full height and glared at the beast. The king opened his mouth, displaying his own savage teeth. 'Tell me why I should deal with you animals?' he hissed.

'Because we have something you want,' the Gor Allta said. 'We have the Grey Warrior.'

'We don't want her,' Morc said to the beast-man.

The Gor Allta's smile broadened. 'We understand she is close to the Emperor. How will he feel if he knows you allowed us to feast off one of his favourites.'

'How do I know you have not already eaten her? Let me see her,' Morc demanded. Without turning his head, he hissed to Cichal. 'Take as many troops and nathair as you need. Circle around behind the islands and come at this group from the rear. Snatch the woman warrior and bring her here. Then, you can carry out the Emperor's command and teach these beasts a lesson they will never forget.'

Cichal bowed and walked away without another word. He was met at the entrance to the caves by a breathless Fomor who told him of the human-kind's escape. Cichal looked at the officer in astonishment. Even in the heart of the Fomor palace, they had managed to escape: it was unbelievable!

'Should I tell the king?' the Fomor asked.

'Not yet,' Cichal snapped, turning away. 'The humans are trapped; they have nowhere to go.' He continued on down through the tunnels into the nathair nests. Balor had told him that the red-haired humans were from a Time to Come, a time when the human-kind completely ruled the earth and there were none of the Fomor or the were-folk in the world. He hadn't really believed him, but now, having seen them in action, having see their cunning and resourcefulness, he was willing to believe it. Maybe the Emperor was right; maybe the only way for the Fomor to survive on this world was to destroy the entire human-kind race. He heard shouts from the Gor Allta and realised they were bringing Scathach.

Two of the Gor Allta hauled the Grey Warrior to the bridge.

'She is still safe, Fomor,' the Gor Allta said. 'But the sun will soon be sinking and we will be assuming our were-shape. I cannot guarantee her safety then.'

'What do you want?' Morc asked.

'You have one of our tribe. We will trade the grey woman for our tribesman.'

'I will think on it,' Morc said, turning away and striding back across the bridge, leaving the Gor Allta — and Scathach — staring at him in amazement. The king was hoping that the Gor Allta would not retreat into the jungle for the night, but would camp around the bridge, awaiting his answer.

'Bring me the Gor Allta prisoner,' he said to the Fomor officer waiting in the cave mouth. Morc's tongue flickered, tasting the unusual odour of a Fomor's fear on the dry air. 'What is wrong?'

'The human-kind prisoners have evaded us lord. They tricked us on the bridge to the dungeons, and then cut it. They are trapped,' the Fomor continued quickly, 'but we cannot get across to them at the moment.'

'Why did you not send an officer across first to wait for the prisoners?' Morc asked quietly.

The beast shook his head. 'They were human-kind ... whelps...' he began.

'You have failed me,' the king continued. He strode into the tunnel, the slithering of his tail the only sound in the silence.

The Fomor Officer allowed himself a quick smile of relief. Maybe the old king was getting soft, and weak. The punishment for failure was usually death. The officer's grin grew wider as the king disappeared into the darkness. Maybe it was time to think about choosing another ruler.

Morc's voice drifted back down the tunnels. 'Officer. You know the punishment for failure. Throw yourself off the edge of the bridge!'

The timing would have to be just right Cichal realised, as the nathair soared up out of the cave. Behind him, in a long snaking line, a hundred black fighting nathair followed him out into the darkening sky. This was one of the few times the nathair could fly over water; when the sun was sinking in the west and the waters below were smooth and dark, throwing up no reflections to confuse the light-sensitive flying serpents.

Cichal brought his troop around the headland, flying into the east. They kept low in the sky, keeping the islands between them and the forest. The sun finally sank as they rounded the second of the smaller Fomor isles, then turned and headed back towards the Forest of Caesir.

The nathair had now drawn up into a triangular formation with Cichal at the lead. He brought his Troop in low across the trees, the only sounds in the night sky the faint clapping of the creature's wings. He spotted the Gor Allta's night fires scattered along the beach, some of them even burning on the bridge itself.

But where was Scathach?

Cichal's tongue flickered, attempting to sort through the mixture of scents: the mud and greenery of the lush forest, the salt of the sea, the muskiness of the beast folk ... and there, the sharper odour of salt human sweat! His single yellow eye narrowed, and then he spotted Scathach. She had been bound to a tree in the midst of the Gor Allta encampment. He saw her raise her head and look up, her battle senses warning her that something was amiss. When she spotted the shapes in the night sky, her lips parted in a savage smile.

With a wave of his arm, Cichal ordered the Fomor down.

The Fomor had the advantage of surprise. They crashed into the Gor Allta camp, bringing it awake in a confusion of shouts and cries. The beast-men were terrified of the huge creatures falling from the skies, stone swords flashing, crossbow bolts and arrows screaming through the night, the nathair hissing madly, the Fomor howling.

Cichal dropped to the ground beside Scathach. He slashed the ropes binding her to the tree with his claws and then almost threw her onto the back of his nathair. A Gor Allta loomed up out of the darkness, wrapping its incredibly powerful arms around Cichal, its huge teeth snapping at the Fomor's throat. Cichal's armoured tail snapped around, catching the beast-man in the back of the head, the blow stunning him.

Cichal vaulted into the wooden saddle, urging the nathair upwards.

'I thought nathair couldn't fly at night,' Scathach shouted over his shoulder.

'Neither did the Gor Allta. That's why they weren't expecting us. Usually the nathair need light, but right now they can smell their nests; that's where they'll fly to.'

Cichal and Scathach spiralled upwards into the sky, followed by the nathair, rising up out of the devastated ruin of the Gor Allta camp. Fires were burning in a dozen places.

'Did you see the bard, the Windlord and the beast?' Cichal asked.

'They went to the isle with the others,' Scathach shouted.

'We captured three. But not the bard, the Windlord, nor the Torc Allta. We thought they had remained behind with the Gor Allta.'

'They must be free on the island. But at least you have some of the renegades,' she added.

Cichal shook his head. 'They've escaped,' he said quietly, the wind whipping away his words.

'I don't believe it,' Scathach called. She pounded Cichal's shoulder in frustration. 'This has gone far enough. This time they must be slain on sight.'

The Fomor nodded. 'This time, I agree with you.'

A series of broad stone steps led down into the tunnels. Ken and Ally waited while Megan crept ahead. They were still shaky after their experience on the bridge, the muscles in their legs were aching and Ally's hands were raw where she had gripped the rope sides of the bridge.

'I've never been so frightened in my life,' she whispered.

Ken nodded. He knew what she meant. 'But we did it,' he said. 'We could do it again.'

'You could,' Megan said, trotting back up the steps. 'You faced your fear. Any fear may be conquered by facing it, seeing it for what it is.' She turned back down the steps. 'These are the dungeons. There doesn't seem to be any of the Fomor about.'

Ken and Ally followed Megan down into the dungeons. Here the wall carvings had grown smooth and flat with age, and the glowing fungus had almost completely faded away. Two burning torches set high on the walls, cast a flickering light across the long narrow tunnel. There were six doors on either side of the tunnel, but only two were locked.

Standing on her toes, Megan peered through a viewing slit into the first room. The cell was in darkness and she could see nothing. 'Bring me a torch,' she said, glancing over her shoulder at Ken.

Ken lifted one of the torches out of its circular holder, hissing as the hot metal burnt his fingers. Holding it behind Megan's head, it cast a dim light into the cell. The room was bare except for a stone block set up against the far wall. There was a bulky shape lying on the stone bed. It stirred when the light flooded into the cell, grumbling in its sleep. And then it moved suddenly, rolling off the stone bed, re-appearing before the door. Megan jerked her head back so quickly that some of her hair frizzled in the torch Ken was holding. The face that peered out of the cell was that of a beast, savage and hairy with deep-set black eyes and long yellow teeth.

'Gor Allta,' Ken whispered, recognising the creature. 'You're the Gor Allta prisoner.'

The beast pressed himself up against the door, tilted his head to look at the three humans. He grunted, the sounds almost understandable.

'We've just come through the Forest of Caesir,' Megan said quickly. 'The Fomor pursued us, but your Gor Allta brothers helped us. We were captured but we managed to escape.'

The beast grunted again. A short, black-nailed stubby finger appeared in the little viewing window and pointed downwards. Ken lowered the light. The cell was secured with a thick bar that was lowered into clips which prevented the door from opening outwards. The boy glanced at the warrior maid. 'Do we let him out?' he whispered.

'The Fomor's enemies are our friends,' Megan said quickly. She gripped the bar and attempted to push it upwards. It wouldn't move. Ken put the torch on the floor, and then both he and Megan attempted to push the bar up. But it was too heavy.

Megan then put her back to the door, so that the bar was across her shoulders. Ken and Ally positioned themselves either side of the bar. 'When I say push,' Megan said, 'I want you to push with all your might. Now, ready..? Push!' The warrior maid straightened her legs, taking the weight of the bar across her shoulders, while Ken and Ally pushed the bar upwards. This time it moved. Megan gritted her teeth and heaved again. The bar rose upwards. Ken and Ally pushed harder ... and the bar, which was now at an angle, simply slid out of its clips and clattered to the floor. Megan staggered away from the door and pressed her aching back against the wall. She didn't think she'd ever walk straight again.

The cell door opened and the Gor Allta lumbered out. He was bigger than any of the beast-folk they had so far encountered. His hair was long and shaggy, and when he walked, his knuckles brushed the ground. He stopped before the three children and grunted.

'I think he's saying thank you,' Ken said.

The Gor Allta grunted again.

'He *is* saying thank you.'

Megan staggered over to the second cell. Holding the torch high, she peered inside and discovered a small dark-skinned woman sitting on the stone bed, a young boy and girl held in her arms. They were staring at the door, their eyes wide and frightened. Ally pressed her face to the grill. The resemblance to Colum was startling, the same long dark hair, the same dark eyes. 'Colum sent us,' she said. 'We've come to get you out.' She looked over her shoulder at the Gor Allta and tapped the bar. 'Could you..?' she asked.

The beast man caught the bar in one hand, heaved it away, and pulled open the door.

The small woman and the two children stepped out into the corridor. The woman was slightly smaller than Ally. 'Colum is safe and well?' she asked immediately, her accent gentle and whispering.

'He was in good health when we left him,' Ally said, 'but I don't think he is safe. We came here to rescue you. I am Ally, this is my brother Ken and this is Megan. I don't know the Gor Allta's name,' she added.

'He is Nommo, lord of the Gor Allta.'

'I thought the Gor Allta didn't given their names,' Ken said.

'We both thought we were going to die, so keeping our names secret didn't matter. I am Anu, and these are my children, Er and Eri. We are the last of the Earthlord clan.'

'Do you know of any way out of here?' Megan asked.

'This is a dead end,' Anu said. 'Whenever we have been brought before Morc, it was always across the rope bridge.'

'I'm afraid we've cut off that escape route,' Ken said, lifting the knife, smiling at the unintentional joke.

Anu bowed her head. 'Then we are trapped. There is no other way across the chasm.'

Megan walked back up the steps to the edge of the gap. A warm, foul-smelling wind blew up from the depths, stinging her eyes, making them water. There was no way across the chasm, no way up or down.

Ally stepped up behind her. Holding tightly to the warrior maid's arm, she stared down into the pit, her red hair blown up around her head in long streamers. 'Are we trapped here?' she asked numbly.

Megan nodded. 'Unless the Fomor rescue us, we will die here. We will probably starve to death,' she added.

'I've never seen anything like it,' Faolan said, peering through the trees.

And even the bard, who had seen many of the wonders of the De Danann Isle, could only nod in agreement.

They were crouching at the edge of the forest, staring up at the mountain that dominated the heart of the island. Much of the mountainside had been terraced and cleared for growing grapes, but the centre of the mountain, where the rock was sheer white stone, had been carved and shaped into the likeness of a Fomor's face. The enormous carving was perfect in every detail, even down to the scales around the eyes, the jagged teeth and the forked tongue.

'It is probably Quataz, the Fomor serpent god,' Paedur murmured, squinting up at the carving, wondering how high it was. It seemed to take up most of the cliff-face. 'It's also very old,' he said. 'See how all the sharp edges have been blunted and dulled with age.' He was looking at the great gaping cave that was the mouth when he saw the thin curl of smoke twist out, grey-white in the dawn light.

'Windlord,' he murmured, 'use your senses. Can you tell me what the smoke is composed of?'

Faolan raised his face to the wind, allowing it to flow off his skin. Unconsciously, his tongue flickered as he tasted the wind. Then he grimaced with the odours. 'It's bitter and burnt. Rotten eggs. The Fomor snake scent.' He paused and added quietly, 'And maybe human sweat?'

'Are you sure?' Paedur asked eagerly.

Faolan shook his head. 'No, I'm not.' He attempted to filter out the other wind-borne odours, concentrating on the faint scent of salt on the air. It wasn't sea-salt — he knew that odour — it was drier, sharper ... and it was definitely coming from the face of the carving. 'It could be human sweat,' he said finally.

Paedur looked at the carving again, his dark eyes tracing a path up the cliff-face to the Fomor's mouth. He frowned, desperately trying to remember the little he knew about the Fomor race. They were a secretive, almost mysterious race. Savage and warlike, they lived by a rigid code of honour and they possessed great skills in working stone and leather. They were not were-folk — half-human, half-beast — another race entirely, which had lived alongside the human-kind for thousands of generations. At one time the serpent folk had controlled an empire that dominated the world and enslaved the human-kind. They had ruled by fear, and had insisted that all their subjects worship Quataz, the Feathered Serpent. Paedur nodded, suddenly remembering. At one time they had offered sacrifices to their god ... by feeding the victims to the Stone Face. Shading his eyes with his single hand, he stared at the carving again, and this time noticed the black staining around the mouth.

'I've got a horrible feeling you want to climb into that carving,' Faolan said.

The bard nodded. 'I think it may lead into the Fomor tunnels.'

'We could use my magic,' Faolan suggested.

Paedur shook his head. 'Not yet. You're tired, you haven't eaten or slept. I would imagine you'll be able to call upon the windlore only once before exhaustion takes you.'

'You're right.'

'Save your strength then. We're going to need your magic before too long.'

The sun rose as they reached the foot of the cliff. The small pig, who had been racing ahead, suddenly stumbled, then tumbled head over heels as the were-change shuddered through it. When Paedur and Faolan reached it, the pig had transformed into Ragallach. The bard stretched down his hand and hauled the Torc Allta to his feet.

'It's good to have you back, my friend,' he said. He jerked his head up to where the carving towered over them. The white smoke was clearly visible now, a continuous trickle from between the stone Fomor's gaping mouth. 'Now use that sensitive nose of yours; tell us what you smell.'

Ragallach raised his head, his snout wrinkling. 'I can smell burning rock and the odour of many Fomor.' His savage teeth bared in a quick smile. 'And I can smell Ken and Ally and Megan. There are others with them; I can smell three strange human odours, and a beast smell.'

'We have to get up there,' Paedur said, looking at the rock again.

'Will you be able to climb with only one hand?' Faolan asked. 'Is it strong enough to hold you?'

The bard lifted his hook, allowing the sunlight to flow down the curved blade. 'This hook is no ordinary metal. It is part of me now ... and stronger than any human hand.'

Although the white stone had looked smooth from the distance, now that they were up close they could see that the rock was scarred and pitted, and covered in a light dusting of white ash.

Ragallach rubbed his paw across the dust and brought it to his snout. 'Fire mountain ash,' he grunted. 'The mouth-cave must lead right into the heart of the island. Be careful,' he added, 'the dust will make the rocks slippery.'

Ragallach went first, easily hauling his bulk up the rock face, moving quickly over the stones. Faolan followed more slowly, testing each hand and foot-hold before he put his weight onto it. The bard came last, using the point of his hook to bite into the soft stone, his dark clothes quickly turning white with the dust. The Fomor's carved scales made climbing easier, and in places it was like a staircase. They discovered nests of peist in some of the darker corners, the tiny serpents hissing madly at the intruders. And once Ragallach put his hand through a damhan's web. The huge grey hairy spider darted for the Torc Allta, its razor-sharp jaws clicking. The Torc Allta took a deep breath and blew a cloud of dust at the creature. It immediately curled up into a tight grey ball. The Torc Allta nudged the damhan to one side and continued climbing.

They stopped on a ledge just below the jutting stone jaw. The rock here was thick with white dust, but even that couldn't conceal the blackened scorch marks. Standing just below the opening they could hear the moaning sighs that came from the mouth. It was only now as they stood right up at the carving that they realised just how big it was. Each of the Fomor's teeth was as tall as Faolan; the mouth was an enormous cavern, and the eyes were deep, dark caves.

Ragallach lifted Paedur up into the stone mouth, and then scrambled up himself, clambering between the teeth. There was a fluttering in the vast cave behind them, and a flight of peist — green and crimson and gold in the morning light — darted out and spun around in the air before they vanished into the forest below. Faolan turned to follow their flight ... and suddenly realised just how high they had climbed. The forest floor seemed very far below. A winking flash of sunlight caught his attention and he was turning towards the light when the clearing below filled up with Fomor. Sunlight flashed again ... and the Windlord realised that it was Cichal's metal eye patch reflecting the light. Scathach was standing beside him, and while Faolan couldn't read the beast's inhuman expression, Scathach's savage grin was triumphant.

The Grey Warrior raised her sword and pointed to the two humans and the Torc Allta on the cliff face. 'Kill them!' she screamed.

A hundred Fomor drew back on their crossbows and bows, took aim — and fired. The hollow headed arrows screamed through the air. Faolan threw up his hands, drawing the wind around himself in an almost visible spinning disc. It sucked the arrows and crossbow bolts into it, pulling them away from Paedur, Ragallach and himself.

The arrows spun in the whirlwind which crushed them to slivers of wood and flattened metal. Splinters rained down on the Fomor.

'Again,' Cichal shouted. 'Keep firing.'

Ragallach leaned out from between the stone teeth. 'Take my arm,' he called.

Faolan reached up and caught the Torc Allta's paw. The beast hauled him up — just as another flight of arrows shattered around the stone teeth.

'This way,' Paedur called from further down the tunnel, his voice echoing off the stone. 'Keep low,' he added as more arrows clattered and shattered off the stones, rattling around the cave. One ricocheted off the stones by Faolan's face, showering him in sparks as he scrambled away.

'We don't know where these tunnels lead,' Faolan whispered. 'We could be walking right into a Fomor trap.'

'We have no choice,' Paedur reminded him.

'No prisoners,' Scathach screamed as half the Fomor troop raced for the cliff face. The remainder kept up a steady rain of arrows onto the Stone Face's mouth. The Grey Warrior turned to Cichal. 'They must be demons.'

Cichal shrugged. He didn't care what the humans were. They were trapped in the mouth. If his troops didn't get them, then the god would speak at noon: and anything in the mouth would be destroyed.

Paedur muttered a word and his hook glowed with a strong yellow-white light. They were standing in a tunnel at the very back of the cave — in the throat, Faolan realised with a shudder. He ran his fingers along the walls. They came away black with grime.

'Soot,' Ragallach said, watching Faolan sniffing his fingers.

The light from the bard's hook suddenly died away. It took their eyes a few moments to adjust to the dim light, and then they realised that they were standing at the edge of a sheer drop. Far, far below, a twisting red line burned in the darkness. There were two pools of light below them, on the left and right hand sides, illuminating two tunnels. And standing in the mouth of the right hand tunnel, with his hands on his hips, staring across the chasm was Ken. As they watched, he was joined by his sister. They were pointing to the opposite side of the gap. Their voices echoed up into the vast cavern.

'You shouldn't have cut the rope bridge,' Ally snapped.

'And if I hadn't, then the Fomor would have caught us.'

'But we're trapped here. There's no way up or down. And I don't think the Fomor are going to rescue us.'

'I think you're right.' Running his fingers through his hair, Ken raised his face to the blackness. 'Where are Paedur and the others?' he asked desperately.

'Right here!'

Ken almost fell over the edge of the chasm with fright. He looked at Ally, not believing his ears. 'Paedur ... Paedur? Is that you, really you?' He twisting his head from side to side, squinting up into the blackness, but he could see nothing.

'Stay where you are,' Paedur's voice was calm and controlled. 'Faolan and Ragallach are with me. We're coming down to you now. There are steps cut into the side of the rock face. Have you found the Earthlord's family?'

The voices had brought the others out of the tunnel. 'Yes, they're safe. And we've found the Gor Allta leader as well.'

'You've done well,' Paedur's voice boomed off the walls. There was a sound of footfalls echoing off stones.

'Where are they?' Anu asked.

Nommo, who had transformed into his human shape at sunrise, pointed with a hairy arm. His flat face wrinkled as his broad nose sorted through the odours. 'There they are.' He pointed into the darkness above their heads.

'I can't see anything,' Ally said.

'There,' Megan said suddenly, pointed across the chasm. She suddenly started to laugh.

'What's so funny?' Ken demanded.

'Can't you see?' she asked. He shook his head, frowning. 'The steps,' she said. 'The steps come down on the far side of the chasm. They can't get to us — we're still trapped.'

Scathach watched in astonishment as the Fomor retreated from the mouth of the stone idol. There was no sign of the bard or his companions. She rounded on Cichal. 'What's happening? Why are they leaving the cave? What about the renegades?'

The Fomor pointed into the heavens. 'It will soon be noon,' he hissed, as if that explained everything.

The Grey Warrior ground her teeth in frustration. 'What has happened to the humans,' she demanded. 'I thought they were trapped in the idol's mouth, how could they have escaped?'

'There is a tunnel at the back of the mouth. It leads down into the heart of the mountain, where the prisoners are kept. In the old days, prisoners were taken out of their cells and brought up along the tunnel, so that they could be sacrificed to Quataz, the Feathered Serpent.' He pointed with a taloned claw. 'They would be tied to the god's teeth, and there they would wait for the god to speak.'

Scathach shook her head. 'How would the god speak?' she demanded, 'and what has this to do with the humans?'

The beast shrugged. 'The humans are trapped. There is no escape from the tunnels, the only exit is through the Stone Face. Besides,' he added, 'the god will speak at noon. His breath will destroy them!'

Paedur crouched at the very edge of the chasm and peered down into its depths. Faolan stood behind him, while Ragallach took up a position in the cave mouth, in case any Fomor attempted to creep up on them.

Between them, Ken, Ally and Megan had told how they had been forced across the rope bridge and how they had destroyed it, trapping themselves in the process.

'You've got to help us,' Ally finished.

Paedur nodded. His attention was distracted by the river of lava far below. Its smooth red and black surface was broken now by brilliant flashes of yellow light, and the smoke that wafted up the tunnel was thicker, dirtier. He stared hard at the soot darkened walls of the abyss and followed the walls up into the darkness .... He could feel his heart suddenly quickening in his chest: he knew how the walls had come to be coated with black soot! He decided to say nothing, there was no point in alarming everyone. As far as he could see there was only one way to get everyone across the abyss.

Standing up, he dusted off his hands and drew Faolan to one side. 'How strong is your wind magic here?' he asked.

'I don't know,' Faolan said. 'There is some wind blowing up from the pit. I suppose I could use that.'

'Can you shape it?'

'Shape it? How?'

'Into a bridge.' The bard's dark eyes were glittering. 'I want you to create a bridge of air across the abyss. Can you do it?'

The Windlord looked at the distance across the chasm. He had created wind-dragons and ridden on them, but that had been in the open air, with the full force of the wind's power and energy surrounding him. But he wasn't sure if there was enough energy here in the tunnel to create the bridge the bard wanted.

'There is no other way, Faolan,' Paedur said urgently. 'The Fomor know where we are. If we don't get out of here right now, they'll send an army in after us.' He squeezed the Windlord's shoulder. 'You are our only hope.'

The golden-haired boy nodded quickly. 'I'll try.' He moved away and sat cross-legged at the edge of the chasm, with his hands folded in his lap. Closing his eyes, breathing deeply, shutting out all other distractions, all other sounds, he called the wind to him. He didn't even hear the bard call across the gap.

'We can get you across,' he began, but then stopped as a long finger of fire erupted up from below. It splashed off the walls of the chasm and dripped slowly back down again. 'You have to trust us,' he continued. 'You have to believe in us. You have to believe in yourselves.'

Smoke was now rising thickly from the river of molten rock below, and streamers of fire were spitting upwards.

'Faolan is going to create a bridge of wind and air across the chasm.' He saw the look of alarm on Ken and Ally's face and tried to reassure them. 'You know how powerful Faolan is. You've ridden the wind-dragon. You simply have to believe that he can do this. You have to believe you are walking across a bridge.'

'I believe he can do it,' Ally called across, 'I just don't think I can do it.'

'Nor I,' Ken said, staring down into the pit. 'What's happening to the lava below?' he asked, 'why is it popping and bursting like that?'

'I would guess that it's getting ready to erupt,' Paedur said calmly.

The outline of a bridge appeared across the abyss. Grey and ghostly, it was nothing more than a flat path, without sides or rails and looked no more solid than smoke. It slowly solidified as Faolan concentrated on it, his eyes squeezed tightly shut. He was afraid to open his eyes to look at it just in case his own disbelief would destroy it. His lips moved, breathing an almost silent, 'Now!'

'Now,' Paedur commanded.

No-one moved.

'Now!' Paedur ordered, using his specially trained tone of command.

Anu stepped up to the edge of the bridge of wind and smoke. She knelt beside her children and tore the hem off her dress. Making two blindfolds, she covered Er and Eri's eyes. Taking her children by the hand, she fixed her eyes on the bard ... and strode out across the abyss. She paused, feeling solid wooden boards, rough and raw, beneath her bare feet.

'Come to me,' Paedur said quietly. 'Just look at me.'

Anu and her children walked across the gulf.

Paedur could clearly see the shape of the bridge, and Megan and Nommo could also see it, because they believed in magic: they knew it worked. But Ken and Ally could see nothing beneath the woman's feet; they saw her walking across thin air.

Anu, Er and Eri reached the far side of the chasm and stepped onto the stone ledge.

'Quickly,' Faolan breathed. Sweat was pouring down his face, and the muscles of his jaw were tight with tension.

There was a rumble deep in the earth and then a long finger of fire spat upwards from the river of lava. The air was suddenly foul with the smell of rotten eggs.

Without hesitation, Megan strode across the bridge of air and stepped onto the ledge. It was only when she reached the far side that she began to shake, her hands trembling uncontrollably.

More and more vibrations were shuddering through the ground, churning the river of lava into a frenzy of fire. Huge bubbles formed on its surface. When they burst, they sprayed lava high into the air, some of it coming dangerously close to the ledge.

Faolan was shaking with the effort of holding the bridge together. Paedur went and stood behind him, resting his single hand on the boy's shoulder, pouring some of his own strength into him. 'Now!' the bard commanded. 'Come across the bridge now.'

Ken and Ally looked at one another, each seeing fear mirrored in the other's eyes. Nommo rested his hairy hands on their shoulders. 'You must go,' he grunted.

Ken shook his head. 'We can't.'

'We can't see any bridge...' Ally began.

'The bridge is there,' Nommo insisted. 'I will walk across it,' he continued. 'Just watch me. Follow me.' The Gor Allta squeezed their shoulders and walked onto the bridge of air. He turned to look back at them. 'Watch me. Look at me. Follow me.'

'Quickly,' Paedur shouted. 'We don't have much time.'

Ally reached for her brother's hand. It was damp with sweat and although it was now hot and sticky in the tunnels, his skin — like her own — felt cold. Without a word, they both stepped off the ledge into the air.

It was solid beneath their feet.

Nommo bared his yellow teeth in a savage smile. 'Follow me.'

'... five ... six ... seven ....'

Ally was counting, and Ken could feel his heart pounding in unison as she counted every step. He kept his eyes fixed on the Gor Allta, concentrating on him, seeing only the beast-man's face, his coarse hair, his broad, flattened nose, his strong yellow teeth. But at the back of his mind, he knew that if he were to look down, he would see himself standing in mid-air, with long streamers of fire splashing up on the walls below, some of them coming close enough to singe the soles of his feet.

'... fifteen ... sixteen ... seventeen....'

He could feel his sister's grip tightening on his hands, squeezing his fingers painfully together, and he knew he was clinging to her hand with equal intensity.

'... twenty-five ... twenty-six ... twenty-seven ....'

The Gor Allta stepped up onto the ledge, then turned and stretched out his hands. 'Come to me.'

It was three more steps to the stone ledge. Ken turned to look at his sister, his face beginning to relax into a smile. She looked at him and smiled back ... and in that instant their concentration was lost. They felt the bridge of air dissolve beneath their feet as they started to sink.

Nommo lunged forward and caught the front of Ken's shirt, hauling him forward onto the ledge with bruising force. Ken was still clutching Ally's hand — but she didn't make the ledge. She slammed into the wall beneath, winding her. She couldn't even scream. Only her brother's grip was keeping her from plummeting to the lava below. She felt as if her arm was being torn from its socket ... and then she felt her sweaty fingers begin to slide off Ken's hands.

Nommo and Ragallach's heads appeared over the edge of the ledge. They grasped her arms in paws and hairy hands and lifted her straight up onto the ledge. She swayed for a moment and then fell to her knees beside her brother. His eyes were bright with tears. 'I thought I'd let you go.' He lifted his hands, and she could see where her nails had cut deeply into his flesh.

'Let's go. Everyone off the ledge,' Paedur commanded.

They barely made it off the ledge before the lava erupted from below in a series of shuddering explosions. The flames washed up the walls, bathing the ledges in liquid fire,

Cichal's tongue darted, tasting the sulphur on the air. He looked up at the stone face just as long streamers of flame spat from the mouth, flickering like a fiery serpent's tongue.

'The god has spoken,' he said to Scathach. 'The renegades are dead.' He wondered why he couldn't smell burnt meat on the air.

Balor strode across his huge map of the De Danann Isles in a foul humour. Over the past few days more and more reports had come in of rebellious cities and towns. They were refusing to pay taxes or send him tribute and some of the western cities had even declared themselves independent of the empire.

Balor hissed. The humans had seen that he could be defeated and that had made them brave. They thought him weak. Perhaps it was time to teach them a lesson they would never forget. Without turning around, he snapped, 'Bring me the Earthlord.'

The Fomor standing to attention at the door saluted and left.

With the tip of his sword, Balor drew a ragged line down the western side of the De Danann Isle, from the city of Murias to the ruin of Gorias. Then, in a sudden fit of temper, he slashed at the map to the left hand side of the line.

When Colum was brought into the room, he found Balor staring at the ruin of his model map. The Emperor pointed with his sword. 'Together, you and I will work the most powerful magic ever created on this island,' he hissed. 'I want you to use your earthmagic to tear away this land from the rest of the De Danann Isle. Its people do not wish to be part of my empire ... and I do not wish them to be part of the De Danann Isle!'

The young Earthlord looked at the line Balor had drawn and then shook his head. 'It is too much. I haven't the strength to do it.'

Balor rounded on him, the human side of his face twisted into a savage mask. 'I will give you the strength to do it. I will lend you my strength.'

Colum looked at the map again, and swallowed hard. Balor was asking him to cut right through several hundred leagues of land — jungle, desert, rich grassland. He shook his head. 'I can't do it. It will disturb the balance of nature. Who knows what will happen to the rest of the De Danann Isle if I create such destruction? Who knows what will happen to the rest of the world?'

Balor leaned forward, and the boy saw his own distorted reflection in the Emperor's metal mask. 'Just do it,' he hissed, 'or the Fomor will feast on your family.'

Colum stared defiantly at the Emperor. 'I will do it on one condition: you will release my family.'

For a moment, Colum thought the Emperor was going to strike him, but then he simply nodded. 'Agreed.'

'When do you want it done?'

'When is your power at its strongest?' Balor asked.

'Noon.'

'It is past noon now. You will rest and eat. Tomorrow at noon, you will work your magic.'

The renegades moved cautiously down the tunnels. Ragallach carried a semi-conscious Faolan on his shoulders, while Nommo and Megan led the way. Anu and the twins kept close behind, while Paedur followed behind Ken and Ally, who were still shaky from their terrifying experience on the bridge of air.

Nommo held up his hand and waved everyone back. They pressed themselves against the walls as a group of Fomor walked past the mouth of the tunnel. The beast-man popped his head out, checked that the coast was clear, then called them forward. They moved deeper into the Fomor caverns. The walls were brighter now, thickly coated with shining fungus, and the hard-edged Fomor writing was everywhere. Megan called Ally forward and pointed ahead to two tunnels. 'Which one did we come through?' she asked.

She pointed to the right.

The warrior maid shook her head slightly. 'I thought it was the one to the left.'

Ally looked at the tunnels again. They seemed identical. But maybe they had come through the left hand tunnel; she wasn't sure anymore.

Paedur crept forward. 'What's wrong?'

'We can't remember which tunnel we came through,' Megan said.

Paedur shrugged. 'Follow your instincts.'

'Left,' Megan said. Ally nodded.

'Left it is,' Paedur whispered.

This tunnel was larger than the others and was criss- crossed with many smaller tunnels. They raced down it, darting past cave mouths where Fomor families crouched behind bead curtains. Once, they rounded a corner and discovered two Fomor warriors standing with their backs to them. They tiptoed back and slipped down a side-tunnel, just as the two officers turned, their tongues flickering.

'Did you smell something...?' one asked.

'The smell of the human-kind prisoners has lingered on the air,' his companion remarked.

They had almost reached the end of the tunnel when a Fomor stepped into it. They spotted one another at exactly the same time. As he stepped into the light, they realised that it was Cichal.

Ragallach gently laid Faolan on the ground, and then he and Nommo faced the Fomor. Megan took up a position beside them, wishing she had her blow pipe, but she was armed only with the knife Ken had taken when they'd landed on the isle.

Paedur walked forward and faced the Fomor Officer, who was staring at them, his hands on his hips. Cichal still hadn't drawn his sword.

The beast bowed slightly. 'You should have been consumed when the god spoke with his voice of fire,' he hissed, 'but somehow I'm not surprised to find you still alive.'

'It seems the gods are with us,' Paedur said simply.

Cichal nodded his great head. 'I can believe that. What are your plans?'

The bard shrugged. 'To escape. To return to Falias. To defeat Balor. But you know all this,' he added, 'so I am telling you nothing new.'

Cichal turned his head to look behind him. 'We are alone,' he hissed, 'so we can speak freely. The human-kind and the Fomor have been enemies from the dawn of time. But we have some foes in common. And lately I have come to think that we should unite to defeat the common foe: Balor.'

'It is a trap,' Nommo grunted.

Paedur shook his head slightly. There was no reason for Cichal to lie to them. He was a highly trained Fomor Officer, armed with a sword and his own natural weapons, his teeth, claws and lethal tail: if he wanted to he could have slain them all. Or he could have simply called for assistance. But he had done neither. 'Why should we trust you?' he asked.

'Because I believe in the gods. You survived all that the Emperor, Scathach and I sent against you: you must have had the gods on your side. Lately, I have come to realise that Balor is mad. Perhaps it is his mixed blood; perhaps the hideousness which makes him cover his face has driven him mad.' Cichal held up a sliver of carved wood. 'This arrived a while ago from Falias. At noon tomorrow, Balor will force the Earthlord to cut away the entire western seaboard from Murias to Gorias.'

Anu pushed her way forward to stand beside Paedur. 'But he can't do that. The sudden release of energy will destroy the entire island, probably sink it into the ocean.'

Cichal nodded. 'That is what I feared.' The Fomor stepped aside. 'Go now. Do what you have to do.' He pointed with a long-nailed claw. 'The nathair nests are down that tunnel. There is a large, ugly, grey-skinned beast there. It is mine. It is strong and tireless. It will carry you back to Falias.'

Paedur walked up to the Fomor and stretched out his hand. The beast looked at it for a moment and then he clasped it in his claw. 'We will meet again, Cichal,' Paedur said quietly.

Scathach stood before Morc, the Fomor king. 'I insist that we look for their bodies,' she snapped.

Morc glared at the woman, his tongue beginning to flicker madly. 'You are my guest here,' he hissed. 'And my guests do not insist.'

The Grey Warrior bowed her head. 'I spoke rashly. Insist was not the correct word. I would like your permission to search the tunnels to bring back some evidence that the renegades have been destroyed.'

'Nothing could have survived the god's breath,' Morc said reasonably.

'These have survived worse,' she said simply. 'I must bring the Emperor proof that they are dead.'

Bored by the woman, the Fomor king turned away. 'Take a dozen warriors,' he said finally. 'Search the tunnels.'

The stench from the nathair nests was overpowering. 'Breathe through your mouths,' Anu advised her children.

Ally followed her advice, and then discovered that she could taste the serpent-odour on her tongue.

They were standing in the entrance to an enormous cavern, which was riddled with hundreds of caves. And each cave held a single nathair. Some wore their hoods and seemed to be sleeping, but others were hissing madly at their neighbours, jaws snapping. The cavern took the sounds and magnified them, until it seemed as if the cave was full of whispers.

Ragallach put his paw on Paedur's shoulder and pointed. On the other side of the cave, a Fomor was sitting on a squat stone seat. His head was nodding forwards onto his chest, and he seemed to be sleeping. On the walls behind him were eight flat stone keys. The Torc Allta pointed to the nearest nathair nests. Paedur saw that the serpents were chained into their caves. He looked at the keys again, squinting hard in the dim light. The keys seemed identical, so probably any key would open the chains.

Ragallach pointed again. On the opposite side of the cavern the nesting caves were larger. Two held enormous black nathair, and in one a grey nathair slept.

Paedur stepped back into the tunnel and turned to the group. 'We have to cross the cavern to get to Cichal's grey nathair. There's one Fomor, but he seems to be sleeping. We're going to form a single line and then walk right down the centre of the cave. I'll go first and get the key from the wall behind the guard. As soon as I get it, I want you to start moving.' He looked at Faolan. 'How do you feel?'

'The smell woke me,' the Windlord whispered, his voice hoarse and raw. 'I'm just tired,' he smiled.

Paedur nodded. He turned to Ken who was staring in horror at the hundreds of nathair. This was his worst nightmare. 'I can send you to sleep,' the bard said quietly, 'make you walk across the cavern without seeing the serpents.'

Still looking at the nathair nests, Ken shook his head. 'If I can defeat my fear of heights, I can overcome my terror of snakes.'

The bard nodded. 'As you wish.' He abruptly turned and darted across the cave, his booted feet making no sound on the stones.

Some of the nathair spotted him, and their long necks poked out of their caves, following his progress.

There was no wind in the cavern, so Paedur was unsure if the sleeping Fomor would be able to smell his human scent as he stepped around him. The bard looked at the stone keys before he touched them: they were identical. But just to be on the safe side, he took all eight. Stepping away from the Fomor, he raised his hand high, waving his companions on.

As soon as they stepped out into the cavern, Megan in the lead, Ragallach and Nommo taking up the rear, all the nathair woke. Their heads darted out of their caves, mouths opening and closing, tongues flickering madly as they attempted to identify the source of the strange odours.

Paedur ran for the grey nathair's cave. It was awake, but its heavy hood prevented it from seeing what was happening. The creature was secured by a thick stone chain to a loop in the walls. Stepping up to the serpent, the bard fitted the first key into the lock and turned it. The chain fell away. He was turning back to his companions, a smile of triumph on his face ... when Scathach and a dozen Fomor raced into the cavern!

Scathach screamed her terrifying war cry as she dragged her two swords free. All the nathair immediately broke into a frenzy of hissing, crying, calling. Their heads darted out of the caves, jerking against their chains.

Ragallach and Nommo turned to meet the Grey Warrior who was charging across the cavern, but Faolan stepped in front of them. 'Get onto the grey nathair,' he said tiredly. 'I'll hold them back.'

Paedur came and stood behind the Windlord. 'You're too weak to do this,' he said.

'Do we have a choice?' Faolan asked. Without waiting for an answer, he said, 'Lend me some of your strength, Paedur.'

The bard put his right hand on the Windlord's shoulder, and then Faolan raised his hands — and called the wind!

For a moment it seemed as if nothing was going to happen. Scathach had almost reached the Windlord — her swords were pointed towards him — when she felt the first icy touches of a breeze on her face.

Then the wind came. It howled around the cavern, shrieking madly, the sound actually terrifying the nathair into momentary silence. The Grey Warrior stopped as if she had run into a wall. Her hair and clothes were whipped back, and one of her matched swords went tumbling from her hand. Leaning forward into the howling gale, she attempted to reach the Windlord and bard. But the wind simply plucked her away, spinning her like a leaf, sending her tumbling round and around on the stone floor.

The sleeping Fomor was picked up and tossed through the air. He went crashing into the Fomor warriors, toppling most of them to the ground. The air was filled with straw and twigs from the nathair nests; stones and pebbles were pulled from the ground, then fired through the air like slingshots. One of the Fomor, armed with a crossbow, managed to fire off a single shot, before he lost his footing in the gale. The crossbow bolt flew almost slowly through the air ... then it stopped, flipped over and shot back towards the cave mouth.

'Come on Paedur,' Ragallach called from the back of the enormous grey nathair. The serpent's hooded head was twisting from side to side, trying to make sense of what was happening around it. Although it could smell the other nathair's scents of fear and anger on the air, it didn't know what had frightened them.

Paedur stepped away from the Windlord. And the wind immediately died. Paedur caught Faolan as he fell and half-carried, half-dragged him back into the nathair nest. Nommo reached down and hauled the unconscious Windlord up. The bard hopped up and tapped the Torc Allta on the shoulder. 'Let's go.'

'Where to?' Ragallach called.

'We'll return Nommo to the Forest of Caesir. Then we head for Falias.'

Ragallach nodded, working the reins to allow a little light into the hood. The creature's head immediately turned towards the left.

As they shot out of the cave mouth and into the late afternoon air, Paedur scattered the eight stone keys to the nathair's chains into the forest below.

Standing in the mouth of the Stone Face, Cichal watched the grey nathair struggle to carry its heavy load high into the sky. The Fomor grunted in satisfaction. The renegades had escaped. If anyone could stop the Emperor, they could.

Colum the Earthlord lay on a bed for the first time in many moons. The Emperor wanted him strong when he worked the great magic. Now, having eaten and sat before a warm fire, Colum could feel the tingling earth magic flow into his body, strengthening him. Closing his eyes, folding his hands across his chest, he imagined himself sinking deep into the earth, absorbing its energy and power into him. He examined the earth which Balor wanted him to destroy, working out the stress points, the cracks deep in the heart of the earth, the weaknesses in the strata of rock and mud. He knew he could destroy the land, he knew he possessed the power to open up a crack in the earth that would split the land from north to south.

And he also knew that it would destroy the entire De Danann Isle.

But he had no choice. Not while his mother, brother and sister, remained prisoners of the Fomor.

The boy opened his eyes, feeling warm tears trickling down his face. He wondered where they were now.

They had left Nommo in the Forest of Caesir and had then waited until night fell and Ragallach had changed into his pig-shape before they took to the sky again. Without the weight of the two were-beasts, the nathair flew higher and faster, its leathery wings beating almost silently in the cold night air. Normally, the nathair couldn't fly at night, but Ken had suggested dangling a chunk of luminous wood in front of the creature's hood for it to follow.

Megan now controlled the nathair, while the bard sat behind her, giving directions. Faolan had been strapped to the beast's back. He had been unconscious since he had called the wind, but Paedur said that he was in no danger. Anu sat behind the bard, her two small children asleep on her lap. Ken and Ally sat side by side on the creature's back, with the small pink pig between them.

'How do you feel?' Ally asked.

'I'm OK. Really I am,' Ken said quickly. 'I've just realised that I've been on these creatures three or four times now, but this is the first time I can actually remember.'

'Paedur usually hypnotised you.'

'You know Ally, I don't think I'm afraid of snakes any more.'

'And after what happened in the Fomor tunnels, I don't think I'll ever be afraid of heights again.'

They flew on in silence for a while, until finally, Ken said, 'I sometimes wonder what we're doing here? I mean, all the others have something to offer — skills or strength. What do we have to offer? We've been nothing more than hindrances.'

Ally nodded. She knew what her brother was talking about. They hadn't done much to help this time ... and yet she was coming to believe that they were on the island for a reason. They just hadn't discovered what that reason was yet.

Balor pounded his fists against the table, cracking the wood. The shallow bowl of water slopped over, breaking the magical spell, destroying the image it had just shown. The Emperor swept the bowl from the table with his hand, shattering it on the stone floor.

He had worked a simple spell over the water, curious as to why he had heard nothing from either Scathach or Cichal. But his far-seeing spell hadn't picked up the warrior or the Fomor, instead it had shown him a grey nathair beating its way through the night sky. It was carrying the renegades back to Falias.

So, they had escaped. They had defeated him once before. But they wouldn't do it again. This time he would be waiting for them!

Megan brought the tiring nathair in to land just before the sun rose out of the east. The sudden jolt brought Anu and her children, as well as Ken and Ally, awake. The pig hopped down onto the ground as the first shafts of sunlight broke across the purple sky. The pig shuddered, its muscles twisting and turning as it went through the were-change transformation.

The Torc Allta rose to his feet, yawning widely and stretching to ease his stiffened muscles. 'How far are we from Falias?' he asked.

'Not far,' Paedur said. 'We could see its walls before we landed.'

Ally looked at the bard. 'Do you think Balor will know we're coming?'

Paedur nodded. 'He will know.'

'So are we just going to fly right into his trap?' Ken continued.

'We need to get a message to Colum. We need to let him know that his family are safe. Once he knows that, he can use his power against the Emperor,' the bard explained.

'Is there no magic we can use?' Ally asked.

Paedur shook his head. 'If Faolan were stronger, he could possibly get the wind to carry a message. But any more magic would drain his energy to a dangerously low level.'

'But is there nothing you can do?' Ally persisted.

The bard shook his head again. 'I am only a story-teller. The only magic I have is the little bits and pieces I've picked up in my tales. I have no training and little skill.'

Faolan opened his eyes and looked at Paedur. 'I remember once waking from a deep sleep, hearing your voice in my head,' he whispered. 'It was just before our first meeting in Baddalaur. You warned me that the Fomor were in the town. Could you do that again? Could you get a message to Colum?'

The bard considered for a moment, remembering the time in Baddalaur. But Faolan had only been in the next chamber when he had spoken to him mind-to-mind, while Falias was a smudge of golden walls on the horizon. He nodded suddenly. 'I'll try.'

The bard stood before Anu. Er and Eri hid around the back of her skirts, peering out at the sharp faced boy with the hook where his left hand should have been.

'I'm going to try to get a message to Colum, speaking to him mind-to-mind. But I'm going to need your help.'

The small, dark-skinned woman smiled sadly. 'I have no magic.'

'I simply want you to see your son's face in your mind's eye. Think about him. See him. Can you do that?'

'Of course.'

Paedur reached out and took Anu's small hand in his. Bowing his head, he closed his eyes. 'Think about the Earthlord,' he whispered.

'Colum ... Colum ... Colum.'

Far off in his small bedchamber, the dark-skinned boy turned quickly, thinking someone had come into the small bedchamber. But the door was closed.

'Colum ... Colum ... Colum.'

The Earthlord turned around again, looking up at the high ceiling, the window, back to the door again. Was this some sort of a trick?

'We are coming, Colum. We are coming.'

Colum suddenly found he was thinking of his mother ... and the twins, Er and Eri. The image was so clear, so vivid that he felt he could reach out and touch them. And then other faces swam into view: the red-haired girl from the dungeons, Ally, and her brother Ken ... the boar-man ... the dark-haired maid ... the golden-eyed Windlord, looking weak and exhausted. And the bard. Hard-eyed, sharp-faced, he seemed to be staring directly into Colum's eyes. His lips moved. *'We are coming, Colum. We are coming.'* Then he spoke again. *'Be ready.'*

Balor walked around the tower room, finally coming to a stop before the window that looked out onto the south. They would come from this direction, he knew. Once before they had attacked him in Falias, and then he had depended on magic to protect him. Now he was counting on a thousand warriors, mostly humans, along with the few Fomor that had remained in the capital, to destroy the renegades. His men were all armed with bows and crossbows. Once the nathair was sighted, it would be cut down. There were riders mounted and ready and the chariots were yoked. As soon as the nathair fell to the ground, the riders would gallop out and make sure that there were no survivors.

Smiling broadly, Balor glanced up into the heavens: it would soon be noon. It was time to begin the preparations.

The nathair's wings beat furiously, struggling to carry its burden higher into the thin cold air. 'How much further?' Megan called.

Paedur leaned over the beast's back and looked down onto the capital. They had been flying for most of the morning, first circling around in a great loop that would bring them in from the north, then climbing high into the sky before they flew over the city. He planned to drop down into Falias from above. 'Keep going,' he shouted.

'What-what-what are we looking for?' Ally asked, her teeth chattering madly in the icy air.

'The Earthlord's magic,' Paedur called. 'When Colum uses his power, I'll know where he is.'

'Then what?' Ken asked.

'I'm not sure yet,' the bard admitted. 'But we'll think of something.'

The throne room was bare; even Balor's black throne had been carried outside. Light from the huge circular window streamed into the room, creating a broad circle of light in the centre of the black stone floor. Colum stood in the middle of the puddle of light. He was wearing a white robe, belted around the waist with a white cord and white sandals.

Etched in chalk dust on the black floor was a map of the De Danann Isles. It had taken an artist two full days to draw the detailed map. Now, Balor walked across the floor and dragged the toe of his boot down the western side of the map, smudging the drawing.

'I want everything across this line pushed into the sea. Do you understand?'

Colum nodded.

'I will stand behind you and lend you my strength,' Balor continued.

The Earthlord shook his head. 'No. I don't need your strength just now. Later perhaps.' He raised his head to look at the Emperor. 'And if I do this, you will allow my family to go free?' The mention of his family made him think of them again. He had a sudden image of them on a grey nathair flying over a miniature city. It took him a moment to realise that he was looking down on Falias.

'Do this for me and I will arrange for you to fly to the Fomor Isles to be reunited with your family.'

But Colum knew that the Emperor was lying. Once he had destroyed the western part of the De Danann Isles and wiped out all resistance to the Emperor's rule, Balor would have no further use for him.

But until he was certain that his family were free, what choice did he have? If he disobeyed the Emperor, his family would die a horrible death ... and he would be responsible. Raising his hands high, Colum began to draw the earthmagic into himself.

'I feel it,' Paedur whispered.

Faolan nodded tiredly. Leaning over the edge of the nathair, he pointed downwards into the heart of the city. 'It's coming from there!'

The bard tapped Megan's shoulder. 'Take us down.'

The earthmagic flowed up through Colum, burning through him. He lost all sense of his surroundings. He was aware now of the entire Isle of the Tuatha De Danann, from the icy Northlands to the southern Fomor islands. In that instant, he *became* the island. He was the Earthlord. He gathered the power around him and then he directed his attention to the west coast.

Deep in the heart of the island, the boiling lava and liquid mud began to shiver and move as the powerful elemental magic touched them. Rocks trembled, stones cracked as the power pulled at them. The Earthlord sought out the fractures and breaks deep underground, working out where to unleash his power.

Colum knew what he was doing was wrong. He knew the dangers ... but he had no choice.

'He's in the throne room,' Paedur shouted. He could feel the magic in the air, buzzing around his head like a swarm of angry bees.

But even those with no magical talent could feel the power that flowed around the palace. The very air tasted bitter, and the tired and edgy nathair was becoming harder to control.

'We've got to stop him,' Faolan shouted.

'How?' Paedur called. 'How are we even going to get into the palace?'

Ally leaned forward and tapped the bard's shoulder. 'I've an idea.'

'Now!' Balor screamed. The throne room was trembling with the power that flowed through the boy. Although the Emperor was standing at the other side of the room, he could feel the stones beneath his feet vibrating steadily.

The boy stretched out his hand, fingers spread wide, pointing to the map ...

... And the nathair flew through the circular window in a terrific explosion of glass. The room filled with a haze of tumbling shards of multicoloured glass.

Colum turned. He was shivering madly, the earthmagic burning through his body. He saw the figures on the back of the crazed nathair, saw his mother's face, and then the twins, dazed and wide-eyed.

With a howl of triumph, he turned back to the Emperor, but Balor was already pulling off his metal mask.

Colum released his earthmagic even as he was dropping to the ground. He heard the bard's screamed warning, 'Cover your eyes!'

The nathair's scaled skin cracked and popped as it turned to stone. Its hood had been knocked off when it crashed through the window and its enormous slit-pupilled eyes had fixed on the first human it spotted: Balor.

The door burst open and fifty Fomor raced into the room, bows and crossbows ready. Strings snapped and bows creaked as they fired at the unprotected humans.

Colum's hands moved — and a whole section of the flooring reared up, forming a protective wall in front of the humans. An enormous crack appeared in the floor around the Emperor. And then the roof caved in on top of him, burying him beneath golden stones. The huge blocks in the walls began to explode into dust, leaving gaping holes. In the corridor outside, the black throne melted, the stone running like liquid, turning it into an unrecognisable lump.

Colum rose to his feet. His hair was wild now with the earthmagic and the smile on his face was terrifying. He no longer looked like a boy: he was the image of a powerful god delivering judgement. He turned and strode back to where the humans and Torc Allta were huddled behind the stone nathair. 'We should leave,' he said calmly. Behind him another section of the ceiling fell in.

Balor surged to his feet in a cascade of stones and grit. Fire blazed from his hands, cold balls of fire bouncing around the room, turning stone to liquid where they touched.

Colum's fingers twitched — and the ground opened up and swallowed the Emperor. A portion of the ceiling fell into the hole after the Emperor and then, deep in the heart of the palace, there was a sudden detonation that rocked the building. White smoke curled up through the ragged hole in the floor.

The humans raced through the Emperor's palace, Ragallach carrying Er and Eri, while all around them, walls were caving in, ceilings collapsing, corridors disappearing in thunderous explosions of stone. The entire building was shuddering, vibrating, groaning, moaning and roaring.

Paedur led them through the tall golden doors just before they snapped and buckled, twisting like dried leaves.

Although he didn't have to do any more, Colum turned and used the last of the earthmagic he had gathered, releasing it towards the palace. Cracks appeared in the ground all around the golden building. The cracks grew larger, wider, deeper and then, suddenly, an enormous pit opened up all around the building. The palace sank in an explosion of sound that could be heard as far south as the Fomor Isles.

And then the gaping pit closed, the ragged earth shifting and moving, coming together like a mouth snapping shut.

When the dust had settled it was as if the palace had never existed.

Colum turned and smiled at the renegades. They were all covered from head to foot in white dust. 'Coming through the window was brilliant. It distracted Balor long enough for me to direct my magic.'

Paedur patted Ally's shoulder. 'It was a brilliant plan. I wish I'd thought of it.'

'Are you sure this will work?' Ally asked again.

'It worked before, didn't it?' Faolan said. 'The timewinds will carry you back to your own time,' he explained. 'But this time, I'm going to put you right back in the same place, a few heartbeats later, so it will be as if you never left your home.'

Ken and Ally and their companions were standing on the scarred earth where the Emperor's palace had once been.

'Will we ever see you again?' Ken asked, looking at each of them in turn.

'Perhaps,' Paedur said. 'But even if we never meet again, we will never forget you,' he added.

Ken grinned. 'We'll never forget this, as long as we live.' He held up his right hand. 'And we have this to remember you by.' There was a solid gold ring on his index finger. All the companions wore one — Ragallach wore his around his tusk. Colum had created the rings from the remains of one of the Emperor's golden doors which had escaped the pit.

Ally looked at Megan. 'You taught me to conquer my fear of heights....'

'And don't forget my fear of snakes,' Ken added.

'You overcame your own fears,' the warrior maid said.

'Now, hold hands,' Faolan commanded, 'and close your eyes.'

Ken and Ally tasted cold air scented with herbs and spices. They felt wind plucking at their hair and skin. And they heard the Windlord's last words, 'I think they'll be back.'

Ally opened her eyes. She was back in Ken's bedroom. The contents of the cracked shelves were scattered all around her, the door was a splintered ruin. How were they going to explain this to their parents?

She turned. Ken was standing behind her, looking in horror at the complete destruction of his room. 'We are in deep trouble,' he whispered.

Ally smiled bravely. 'We've faced Balor and his Fomor ... and they were going to eat us — remember. Compared to that, facing up to Mum and Dad will be easy,' she said confidently. 'We'll tell them ... we'll tell them....' Her voice trailed away. What *were* they going to tell them? 'Any ideas?' she asked.

Ken shook his head. They might have been able to explain away a broken window, maybe even the ruined television ... but how were they going to explain how the whole house came to be trashed?

'Burglars,' Ally said firmly. 'We can say someone broke in — which is true,' she added quickly. 'We just won't tell them it was a seven-foot tall green-skinned reptilian warrior.'

Ken climbed over his ruined bed. He leaned out the window and stared into the snow-covered garden. There was nearly two inches of snow piled up on the windowsill. 'Maybe they won't be coming home tonight,' he said, 'that will give us a couple of hours at least.'

But even as he was speaking, headlights flashed across the garden, and they both heard the old car rattling to a halt in the drive.

Ally turned around in a complete circle. 'What are we going to say?' she whispered in panic. 'Burglars. Stick to the burglar story.'

But Ken wasn't listening. He was watching the way the snow melted when it touched his skin, hissing slightly as it turned into water droplets, then turning to steam. When he lifted his hand off the windowledge, he left a burnt and blackened impression in the painted wood.

'Ally...' he whispered.

Ally turned to her brother, and then her eyes widened in horror. Red-black lines were darting across the bare skin of his arms and legs. Sparks crackled in his air, and there was the faintest suggestion of smoke leaking from the corner of his mouth.

A key turned in the lock downstairs. 'Hello ... we're home....'

Ken brought his hands to his face. He could see faint blue flames dancing across the skin, yet he felt nothing, and the flesh wasn't burning. A spark — bright and blue — snapped between his fingers.

'Ally,' he whispered again, 'what's happening to me?

But his sister could only stare in horror as the cold blue-black flames gathered around her brother in a spinning ball. Sparks leapt from the ball onto nearby metal, sparking and crackling around the room.

'Ken ... Ally! Dear God, what's happened here!' Their mother suddenly screamed. 'Ken? Ally?' Footsteps pounded up the stairs.

A warm, herb-scented wind howled around Ally, spinning bed-clothes, books, clothes, shoes, splinters of wood and pieces of the broken door around the girl as she attempted to reach her brother.

'Ally ... I'm falling.' Ken's voice was little more than a whisper.

She touched his fingers — cool and damp despite the flames flowing from them. Ken caught her hand, holding tightly, pulling her with him ... and they were falling, falling, falling....

She remembered letting go of his hand, saw him spinning away from her in a twisting ball of fire ... and then the ground, white and hard rushed up to meet her.

Ally rolled over on her back. There were shapes gathered around her, looking down, but the sun was shining into her eyes, blinding her and she couldn't make out any details. Strong hands caught her, hauling her to her feet.

'I said they'd be back,' Faolan said, grinning widely.

Ally turned round and around. 'Where's Ken?' she cried, 'where's my brother?'

Paedur touched her hand with his hook, the cold metal silencing her. 'Only you came back, Ally,' he said quietly.

'No,' she shook her head quickly. 'Ken was on fire, cold fire. He was pulled back, he dragged me with him. He's here,' she insisted.

'If he's on the De Danann Isle, we'll find him,' Paedur promised.